1

DARK SECRETS FEAR THE LIGHT

ANNA-MARIE MORGAN

ALSO BY ANNA-MARIE MORGAN

In the DI Giles Series:

For my Family

1

THE ASSASSINATION OF KATE NILSSON

A sharp snap of undergrowth. Seven o'clock. Third time she'd heard it. She dropped to her knee and turned, surveying the gaps in the tree-line. Looking. Listening. Silence. No movement.

She picked herself up and carried on running. More sounds. Wood banging against a tree. Like a beater hounding out a pheasant. She kept running, cursing her own breath for drowning out the noises she was straining to hear.

The ground was soft underfoot. Moss. Twigs. Rotting leaves. The occasional branch. Perhaps it was the encroaching darkness. Maybe there was no-one behind.

'Thwip'

She knew that sound and dropped instinctively.

'Thwip'

Someone was firing at her. High-powered rifle. Six o'clock.

She rolled into the ditch, fighting for breath. Perspiration snaking its way down her neck. She snagged on an old bramble. It gouged her as she tried to free herself, tearing her thigh.

The pounding of boots behind. She dragged herself up and ran for it, weaving side-to-side. The last time she'd done that was in Helmand. Her only tour of Afghanistan. This peaceful wood, so close to home, was the last place she would expect to do it again.

She didn't see the branch which caught her foot. Her momentum took her down into the mud. Its thick, sour grittiness invaded her mouth, crunching between her teeth. She spat out what she could and hauled herself up once more, mud-soaked clothing weighing her down.

The dark, velvety menace of the night encroached further.

The stench hit her before she saw the carcass. A sheep had lost its battle with tangled wire and lay where it had fallen - part skeleton, part rotting mass. She shuddered.

Another bullet. Way too close. Was he toying with her? Harder to run now. The undergrowth slushed and snapped beneath her. She drove shaking limbs on. The weakness of futility overwhelming. She had the urge to turn and face her hunter, like the hind slowing for the lion's teeth to sink into her jugular. Get it over with.

SHE PICKED UP A ROCK, holding it tight behind her back. "You." She pushed wayward hair from her face, leaving muddy trails across her cheek.

The attacker stayed silent, rifle strapped to his back, a pistol aimed nonchalantly at her. How dare he be nonchalant?

She spat at the stony face. A pointless gesture, but it

helped her feel better. Hot tears filled her lashes as she teetered between fight and the temptation to beg for her life. She knew in her heart the latter would be useless. His emotionless expression told her all she needed to know.

She threw the rock at that stony face and took off, beginning another winding run. After only a few paces, the gun rang out. It felt like a punch in the back. As she fell to her knees, her lungs failed. The second shot hit near the first. The assassin took time to walk slowly over and finish her off. A callous shot to the head.

YVONNE TAKES THE CASE

Yvonne put the kettle on its stand and switched it on. She'd felt ready for this but was struggling. Perhaps it was the length of time that had passed. Perhaps it was the confines of her sister's home, filled with so many people. Perhaps it was that she still hadn't quite forgiven her mother.

"Are you okay?" Kim asked with quiet concern.

Yvonne nodded.

"Are you sure? You don't look okay."

"I'm sorry, Kim." Yvonne sighed and brushed the hair from her eyes. "I thought I was ready for the big family get-together, but I'm not sure I am."

From the room next door came the strains of the CD player rocking out Christmas carols. The excited whoops of Kim's children, as they played with their gran for the first time, had the DI feeling guilty.

"It's all right, you know. It's all right to be anxious. Give it a chance." Kim smiled and put an arm around her sister's shoulder.

Yvonne's mobile bleated and she smiled an apology

before crossing the kitchen to retrieve it from the opposite counter.

"DI Giles."

"Ah, Yvonne." DCI Llewellyn drew in his breath.

"Is everything okay?" Yvonne asked, despite knowing it probably wasn't.

"I'm sorry to do this to you, but could you come in?"

"Sir?" Perversely, Yvonne felt pangs of regret.

"A young woman, a soldier, has been murdered near Llydiart. Shot in the back and head."

"From behind?"

"Yes."

Yvonne put her hand over the phone, her gaze turning to Kim, who gave her a quizzical look.

"It's a case." Yvonne paused. "They're asking me in."

"But mum..."

"I know."

"The kids'll be gutted, too."

Yvonne raised her phone once more. "Is there anyone else who can take the case?"

"Not with your experience or sensitivity. She was on Christmas leave with her parents."

"I see." The DI gave her sister an apologetic look. "Give me an hour."

Kim turned towards the door and Yvonne walked after her, one hand lightly touching her sister's shoulder.

"I'll be back."

"Yeah?" Kim frowned. She knew very well what her older sister was like when working a case.

"Yes. I've got to talk to a family. Ask a few questions. I can be back tonight. I'm sure after that someone else can lead the team for a few days."

Kim nodded, but her drawn face signalled lingering scepticism.

"I'll go speak to the others." Yvonne gave her sister's hand a squeeze.

TWO AND A HALF HOURS LATER, Yvonne was apprised of the full events by the DCI. Four hours after the call, and she was on her way to the muddy field, which would now be full of SOCO and uniformed officers.

Yvonne let Dewi drive, and waited patiently as he stopped in LLydiart to pick up a paper and snacks. The post office shop in the tiny hamlet was not manned as a matter of course. It took several minutes for a dark-haired, buxom lady to open up and be ready to serve them. Yvonne took a look at her watch and left Dewi talking, choosing instead to get her wellies out of the boot.

Snow had fallen, interspersed with sleet and rain, leaving slushy mud and driven snow piles in random array. The DI was expecting a messy trek to Kate Nilsson's body.

She wasn't wrong. They followed the hedge line and the blue and white cordon of the designated pathway. The latter already well trodden. SOCO were everywhere and rows of officers walked painstakingly at the other end of the field. Dewi and Yvonne accepted the proffered plastic suits and overshoes and took their place behind the photographer.

Pathologist Roger Hanson was hard at work. Yvonne's gaze turned to the blood-soaked, hair of the victim, who lay, face-down in the ditch.

"Shot in the back as she ran away." Hanson's knees clicked as he stood to greet the detectives. "The killer coolly finished her off with a shot to the head. There doesn't appear to be anything under her finger nails and no defensive wounds."

"So, we know she wasn't in a fight with her killer. It wasn't a heated argument." Dewi scribbled hard.

"She was a fit soldier. Took care of herself. Why didn't she take him on?" Yvonne frowned.

"Maybe she didn't see him coming?"

"Or maybe she knew she couldn't win this one." Yvonne knelt, to get a closer look.

Roger Hanson nodded. "This ditch wouldn't be an obvious place for jogging. She'd gotten caught on a bramble. It's still embedded in her jogging bottoms. All the signs are she was being chased. Body temp and rigour-state fit with that scenario. She was suffering from physical exertion."

"Wouldn't she have been exerted anyway, given that she was jogging?" Dewi chewed the end of his pen, flicking it up and down with his teeth.

"Unlikely." Hanson shook his head. "She'd only been out about thirty minutes. Someone so used to jogging would probably not be exhausted in so short a time. Unless she'd tried a faster pace, which I cannot rule out."

Dewi nodded, a thoughtful expression on his face. "Okay."

Yvonne sat back to look at Hanson. "Can we turn her over?"

Hanson checked with the photographer, who nodded. Hanson completed the turn.

The DI's heart banged in her chest. Kate's eyes were wide open. Her mouth was also partially open. The pathologist clicked on his torch and squeezed the victim's face, to peer inside her mouth. Yvonne balked at the matter-of-factness of it.

"She's got mud inside her mouth and grit between her

teeth. She was certainly trying to get away. She'd probably fallen prior to her final drop."

The DI shuddered and scanned the tree-line. "Well, whoever he was, he must have been fit."

"Or she." Dewi corrected.

"Or she." Yvonne conceded. "When we speak to her friends and family, we should find out if she ran with anyone else. They'd still have to go some to outrun a soldier at the peak of physical fitness." She pointed to the cracked watch.

"Five minutes past four," Hanson offered before being asked. "Stopped when she hit the deck."

"Wow." The DI scratched her head. "Ken Davies called the station at four-twenty. She could have been dead only minutes before he arrived. He said he hadn't witnessed her being killed. How did her murderer disappear so quickly?"

"We should speak to Ken Davies, ASAP," Dewi agreed. "He *had* to have seen something."

"Which direction is the farm?" Yvonne asked.

"As the crow flies, it's behind that copse and through the fields," Dewi said, pointing. "Davies was on his quad bike. He could have been back at the farm within five minutes. Definitely within ten."

"So it may have been four-ten to four-fifteen pm when he got here."

"And the quad tracks mightn't be much help." Dewi sighed. "There are numerous sets and hard to say, definitively, which are the most recent."

Yvonne nodded. "I know. But they do follow roughly the same arc, and if those..." She pointed off to her left, "are the incoming, then the killer may have disappeared off into the copse."

"Right." Dewi agreed. "He'd have heard the quad approaching from some distance away."

"Maybe he was wearing camouflage."

Dewi raised his eyebrows.

"Just a thought, Dewi. Just a thought." She pinched her tongue between her teeth. "Okay. Let's get SOCO and uniform to comb that copse. See if we can get a trace on him. Get the dog team up here. The killer may be long gone, but if he's local-"

"I'll get the postmortem results to you as soon as I can." Hanson peeled off his gloves, signalling to his assistants that he was ready for the body to be taken.

Yvonne stared down at the body bag, placed next to the girl. She mused that soldiers might be no strangers to body bags, but not here. Not in a muddy field next to their home.

3

WHO WAS KATE NILSSON

Yvonne and Dewi headed for Mill House, a large cottage near Llydiart, fifteen minutes from Lake Vernwy. Dewi agreed to wait in the car while Yvonne made a sensitive entrance.

It had started to snow again. Small flakes becoming larger ones. The DI looked skyward, listening to the birds as she waited for the door to be opened. The peacefulness of the country dell contrasted vastly with the turmoil in her head, left over from abandoning her own family that morning. She was filled with guilt, relief, and unanswered questions.

A broad, Nordic-looking man in his late forties opened the door. Yvonne knew immediately this must be Lars, Kate's father. The sad heaviness of his expression and his hunched shoulders would be confirmation enough, even if the DI hadn't caught the resemblance to Kate's photograph.

"Mr Nilsson? I'm Detective Inspector Yvonne Giles, Dyfed-Powys Police."

Lars extended a large, warm hand to shake hers before stepping back to allow her into the hallway. On the walls hung a gallery of family photos, over which Yvonne cast a rapid but thorough gaze.

"Can I get you anything?" Lars motioned her into the medium-sized country kitchen. A tearful Mrs Nilsson sipped from a mug while leaning back against a cream-coloured Aga.

"My wife, Hayley." Lars put a hand on his wife's shoulder. "Kate's mum," he added needlessly.

"Mrs Nilsson," Yvonne acknowledged, with a sad smile.

"Hayley," the other mumbled. "The kettle's just boiled." She leaned her chin on her mug, her eyes glazed.

"I'm all right, thank you." Yvonne chose a position at right angles to the couple, leaning against a row of oak cupboards facing the window. "I'm really sorry about your daughter." Yvonne looked from one to the other. "There is no good time to lose someone you love," she said, eyes half-lidded, "but this time of year is..." She sighed.

"I'm angry." Lars folded his arms across his chest, glistening eyes narrowing in his muscular face. "She was afraid. My daughter was afraid."

"Afraid?" Yvonne frowned. "What was she afraid of?"

"Lars..." Hayley put a hand on her husband's arm and the DI could see she had visibly paled. Lars fell silent.

Yvonne shifted position. She realised Kate Nilsson hadn't been the only one who was scared. She didn't push it. Not yet. "What time did Kate leave to go running?" The DI ran her eyes around the kitchen - the tinsel, draped around witty kitchen signs, a tray of mince pies abandoned on the counter - evidence of celebrations interrupted.

"Around three-thirty. I'd just entered my study when I heard the door go." Lars looked up at the clock.

"She gave me a kiss on the cheek as she left." Hayley broke down, her chest heaving as sobs wracked her body.

"She was found by Ken Davies, who was out checking his sheep." Lars pulled his wife into his arms, kissing her forehead as he removed the spilling mug from her grip to place it on the countertop.

"What time was that?" Yvonne checked her notes. "We received the phone call at four-twenty pm. Was that when he found her?"

Lars pursed his lips. "About then, I think. Well, actually it was about four-ish. Mobile signals are semi-precious out here. They come and go like the mists. I think he had to go back to the farmhouse to call you and then call us."

"He knew who she was then?"

"He should. He went to school with Kate."

"She was lying face-down in the ditch. I'm sorry to tell you that, but how could he be sure it was your daughter?"

"Kate ran every day, often twice a day, whenever she was home on leave. She always took the same cross-country route. Ken said he had spoken to her only yesterday." Lars pulled his arms from around his wife who was now much calmer. "She only had two jogging suits with her. She wore one and washed one. Ken would have seen both."

Yvonne nodded. "Is Ken at the farm every day?"

"Pretty much. As far as I know."

Yvonne made a note to visit the farm as soon as possible. "Mr Nilsson-"

"Lars, please."

"Lars. Would you allow me to see Kate's room?"

The deeply sad expression was back. "Of course." And, after a look from his wife, "Could I ask that you not disturb anything unless you really have to?"

"Of course." Yvonne nodded, adding, "My detective sergeant, Dewi Hughes, is in the car outside. Would it be all right to have him accompany me?"

Lars glanced at his wife, who nodded. "Yes, Detective Giles."

"Please, call me Yvonne," she said in soft tones, as she headed for the door. She was glad Dewi would be joining her. She wasn't feeling her best, head still mashed from worrying about her own family.

She found Dewi listening to radio four with the engine running.

"Feeling cold?" She grinned as she got into the passenger seat.

"It's f...f...freezing," he moaned, exaggerating his shivers.

Yvonne gave him a dig in the ribs. "I should have accepted their cup of tea." She put her tongue out. "Anyway, that wasn't a conversation you would rush, even if you needed to."

It was Dewi's turn to grin. "I was fine. Only just turned the engine on, in fact. And that was mostly because I'd steamed up the windscreen."

"I'm going to go upstairs to see Kate's things. I thought you might like to help."

"Lead me to them."

THE DOOR CREAKED. So did the floorboards, as they entered Kate's room. A used towel had been tossed onto the end of a semi-made bed and her hairbrush and mobile phone lay where she appeared to have left them, on the dresser.

Next to the bed, Kate's army kit-bag. On the walls, several photographs of Kate in Afghanistan.

Yvonne took out an evidence bag and a pair of latex gloves, teasing a few strands of hair from the brush and sealing them away. She pressed the button on the front of Kate's mobile, flicking through apps and files.

"Anything interesting?" Dewi was on her shoulder.

"Possibly. Who knows? I'll bag it up. The tech bods can take a look." The DI frowned, as she flicked through the photographs.

"Ma'am?"

She showed the phone to Dewi.

"What am I looking at?"

"It looks like it could be her barrack room. Bed well made. Very tidy. Regimental flag on the wall."

"So?"

"Keep looking." Yvonne flicked through photo after photo. All of the same room, taken from similar perspectives."

"I feel like I'm playing spot the difference." Dewi shrugged.

"Exactly." Yvonne bagged the phone. "Why would Kate have taken so many photos of her barrack room?"

"Maybe she was trying to get the light just right," Dewi offered.

Yvonne pursed her lips. "Maybe."

She wandered over to the photographs on the wall. A smiling, blonde-haired Kate placing her life on the line. Bravely putting herself in harm's way. "She came back home only to lose her life in a muddy field not quarter of a mile from here. Imagine the relief of her parents on her return," Yvonne said out loud, "only to have her brutally taken from them, in a place where she should have felt safe." She sat on the edge of the bed. "Makes no sense."

Dewi took his own photographs of the mural with his phone.

"Thank you, Dewi," she acknowledged, adding, "Lars said his daughter was afraid-"

A knock on the bedroom door had the DI up off the bed, heart beating fast.

When it opened, Lars Nilsson filled the door-frame.

"We're nearly finished." She sounded breathless. "We've taken your daughter's mobile phone. I hope that's okay?"

"You won't delete anything?" Lars appeared unsure.

"I promise we won't do that, Lars. You said your daughter was afraid."

"She was. She was looking into suspicious events at the barracks. She was constantly looking over her shoulder."

"Go on." Dewi stood next to Yvonne, notebook in hand.

"Suicides and strange deaths. Two alleged suicides in five years. Plus other *accidents*."

"You say *alleged* suicides?" Yvonne frowned.

"Well, if three bullets in the head and hanging from a tree, with no ladder and no way to get up there, are suicides..."

"What did your daughter tell you? In what way was she looking into them?"

Lars glanced back towards the stairs. "She'd begun talking to other young soldiers, friends of the deceased. She'd had run-ins with some of her seniors."

The DI flicked a look at Dewi's notebook, checking he was getting it all down. "Lars, may I ask what it is you do for a living?"

Lars hesitated, then, "I'm a photojournalist. Freelance. I sell stories to newspapers and magazines. Mostly based in the UK but, occasionally, those abroad."

"I see." The DI rubbed her forehead, gazing at her shoes. "Did you ask your daughter to look into those deaths?" She raised her eyes to his, looking straight into him. He coloured.

"Lars? Is everything okay up there?" Hayley's voice rang up the stairwell.

"Just coming," Lars called down. "If you've finished?" He looked from Yvonne to Dewi and then back again, his expression closed.

"For now." She nodded. "Thank you."

THE DI WAS silent as she and Dewi left the cottage, heading for the car. Her DS could see she was churning stuff over and waited for her to snap out of it.

"They're hiding something," she said, finally. "And Hayley Nilsson is scared. Dewi, see to it that a marker is put on their address. Any call-outs to be given top priority."

"Will do, ma'am."

4

QUESTIONS AND INTRIGUES

Back at the station, Yvonne examined the items she had collected from Kate's room and prepared the paperwork for forensics. She was still musing over the dozens of photographs on Kate's mobile. Photographs of her barracks room, all showing the same scene. She put a note in with the phone, requesting two copies of every photo.

After a quick coffee and catch-up with DCs Jones and Clayton, she took a deep breath and knocked on the DCI's door.

Llewellyn gave her a warm smile, his eyes searching her face. "How'd it go?"

"It wasn't easy." Yvonne proceeded to fill him in, then added, "Kate was investigating suspicious deaths, at Dale Barracks in Chester."

"Suspicious?"

"Suicides and accidents, that she and her father believed were murders."

"You think her death was related to her investigations?"

"I think she was taken out by another soldier. Perhaps

Cheshire Police would have more information regarding the other deaths. I hope to speak to them in the next couple of days. But I came to ask if I can go further."

"You want to go to Dale Barracks."

"You know me so well, sir."

Chris Llewellyn ran a hand through his hair, lines creasing his forehead. "Investigating the army is usually a fraught affair. Are you sure you can't get everything you need from Cheshire Police?"

"Well, I doubt it. Her investigation wasn't official. She was talking to other soldiers and friends of the dead. I feel I need to tread in her footsteps. Learn the things she learned."

"If they'll talk to you. Talking to the police is a lot different to talking to one of their own."

"She had run-ins with her seniors, according to her father. I don't know which seniors. My best hope is the other young soldiers on the base."

"You'll need clearance." Llewellyn scribbled a few notes in the pad on his desk. "I'll speak to the Colonel of the regiment, Major-General Forster."

"You know him?"

"I was in school with him. My brother is a close friend of his."

Yvonne's eyes narrowed. "You're a dark horse, sir." She grinned. "I'd be really grateful if you could pull a few strings. Get me in."

"You don't go alone. Take Dewi, and get as much as you can in one day."

Yvonne pulled a face.

"Perhaps two. I'll try to get you two days. Everything else will need to come through military police, news archives and Cheshire Police. Is that clear?"

"Crystal." Yvonne nodded, wondering if two days would be anywhere near enough.

"What about the murder weapon?"

"Pistol, we think. Ballistics have what's left of the bullets. That reminds me, I need to ask Jones or Clayton to speak to the pathologist for a final run down before the report comes out."

Llewellyn nodded. "Well, if there's anything else?"

"No, sir. Nothing else." Yvonne turned to leave.

"Oh, Yvonne?"

"Yes?"

"Thank you for coming off leave for this. Merry Christmas."

"Merry Christmas, sir." The DI gave a weak smile, her sister's disappointed face coming vividly back to her.

DEWI WAS WAITING for her as she came out of the DCI's office, a mug of steaming coffee in each of his hands. "Ken Davies is in interview room one. Are you ready?"

Yvonne grabbed one of the mugs and followed him down the corridor.

Ken sat with his arms folded, his face red, his jaw sticking out. The DI offered him her mug of coffee but he waved it away. Dark-haired and twenty-something, he leaned back in his chair. "How long will this take?" He looked at them all in turn. "It's just we've had a problem with the sheep getting stuck down the brook fence and I usually start my rounds in the next half-an-hour."

"We'll be as quick as we can," the DI reassured him, before introducing herself and Dewi for Ken and the tape recorder. "Mr Davies, can you tell us what time you began your rounds on December twenty-second?"

"Err...that would have been about three-thirty in the afternoon."

"Were you on foot?"

"No. I was on my quad bike."

"The whole time?" The DI wondered if the victim and her killer had heard the quad bike coming.

"No, not the whole time. I had to free a sheep from the fence on the south-side and that delayed me a bit. I would normally be back at the farm about four."

"Four pm?"

"Yeah."

"Did you see anyone prior to finding Kate's body?"

Ken looked away to the door. "No."

"You're sure about that?"

"Very."

"How about after?"

"No. I did look around but I could have missed something. I was shaking with the shock. I saw her red jogging suit and thought it was a bunch of old rags, to start with. Then I was just looking at her. I could see she was dead. No movement, see. It was then I ran back to my quad. I was scared that whoever done her in could still be around, like."

"Did you hear any shots?" Dewi leaned in towards Davies.

"Not that I recall. I mean, I hear shots regularly anyway, it being the shooting season. I was on my quad and thinking about Christmas and going to my mum's for dinner. I wasn't really paying attention. I can't believe she's gone. I talked to her only yesterday. She was always pleasant. Who would have wanted to kill her?"

"Quite." Yvonne agreed. "What time did you talk to her yesterday?"

"It was in the morning, about seven-thirty. Funny, she was in almost the same place."

"That was early. Did she vary her running times?"

"No. She ran early morning and late afternoon. Like clockwork, she was."

"And there's nothing more you want to tell us, Ken?"

"Not that I can think of."

The DI wrapped up the interview. Ken was on the suspect list, but Yvonne did not see him as the prime candidate for Kate's murder. He looked like the proverbial rabbit in the headlights, and this crime had taken something darker. Much darker.

SHE DUCKED out of the interview room, heading down the corridor to the coffee area, to make a quick call. She waited an agonising thirty seconds for her sister to answer.

"Kim, how is it going? I'm so sorry to have left like that. How are the children? How's mum?"

"Are you really telling me you didn't want to leave?" Kim sounded doubtful.

Yvonne sighed. "I'll admit I was feeling uneasy. I was in two minds. But when it came to it? No. I didn't want to leave. And I miss the children and you. And I am missing the opportunity to *really* talk to mum."

Kim relented. "Okay. How's your case coming along?"

"Well, it's just getting going, actually. Loads to do over the coming days, but I *will* make time to come and see you guys and talk to mum before she goes back."

"Stay safe." There was genuine concern in her sister's voice.

"I will. Give my love to the kids."

"I will."

Yvonne stared through the window. Another snow flurry had begun. So far, not much was sticking in Newtown. Just as well. She and Dewi would be driving up to Chester the following day.

She felt her focus returning, feeling better having made the call to Kim. Now all she needed was for the DCI to come up trumps with Broderick Forster.

THE DCI HADN'T LET her down. He came to find her in the coffee room, to let her know he had arranged for her to meet the Colonel of the Royal Welsh the following afternoon. "You'll need to be on time and be polite."

"Are you saying you're worried I wouldn't be polite?" Yvonne raised an eyebrow.

"No." Llewellyn rubbed his chin. "Just don't get his back up. How much freedom you have to question people, and who you get to question, will be directly down to him. You don't have jurisdiction there, and you'll be relying on his good will."

"Goes without saying, sir," Yvonne answered in clipped tones.

"Fine. I trust you to not get his back up."

"I'm sure Dewi will keep me on track." The DI grinned. "I thought *I* was the worrier."

"And be careful."

"Sir?"

"Whoever took that girl out is ruthless and calculating.

If he's on that base, he won't take kindly to you poking around and rattling feathers. Be mindful of that, both for yourself and the young soldiers you're interviewing."

Yvonne nodded. "I really don't want to put any more recruits in danger. I'll tread as carefully as I can."

"I know you will." The DCI held the door open. "Make sure you take Dewi with you."

Yvonne nodded again, before striding down the corridor.

5

DALE BARRACKS

The journey to Chester took around two hours. The latter part of the journey felt like a never-ending series of roundabouts. Dewi put music on.

The DI, deep in thought, had been about to ask him to switch it off but thought better of it. He was cheerful, far more cheerful than she felt. She chose not to spoil his mood.

Dale Barracks was situated just off Liverpool Road. Dewi swung a left off a small roundabout and between two large signs.

Dale Barracks lay to the left and Fox Barracks to the right. A large advertisement hung from the railings, promising the learning of new skills while earning money. The DI pursed her lips. Dewi swung a left into the Barracks entrance.

They waited for guard-duty to come and signal them through. The sign next to the hut read '2nd Battalion Royal Welsh'. A row of Land Rovers were parked to their right.

Dressed in desert-camouflage, military fatigues, the guard

finally made his way to them. Sleeves rolled up to his elbows, weapon held loosely across him. He took a good look at their ID. Yvonne mused that he couldn't have been more than eighteen. She wondered, not for the first time, at the huge weight of responsibility these young soldiers had. He appeared confident and efficient, looking them over and examining their vehicle.

"We're here to meet with Colonel Forster," Dewi offered, eventually.

"I know." He adjusted his cap. "I'll call through to the Colonel's office and let them know you're here." He turned his piercing blues eyes on the DI, his face impassive. With a quick nod, he stepped back and allowed them through.

The DI realised they hadn't received instruction on where to go. She needn't have worried, as one of the Colonel's aides came out to meet them. He signalled where he wished them to park, then walked over to shake their hands as they got out of the car.

"The Colonel's office is this way." He held his hand out in the general direction. "Hope your journey was okay?"

The DI smiled at him. "It was, thank you. I'm DI Giles and this is DS Hughes."

"Staff-Sergeant Jones. Welcome to Dale." He had already set off. His highly polished boots click-clacked on the tarmac.

"THANK YOU." Broderick Forster stood, as they entered, dismissing his aide with a nod.

The DI was struck by his height. He had to be at least six-foot-two. She accepted his extended hand with a gentle smile. There was a stillness about him. A quiet intelligence.

His handshake was firm but not controlling. Yvonne approved.

"Please, sit down." He indicated two chairs abutting his desk, which Yvonne and Dewi duly occupied. He sat quietly observing them as the DI cleared her throat.

"Do I address you as Colonel or Major-General?" Yvonne asked, cautiously.

"Brod," he replied coolly, his gaze level.

Yvonne looked down at her notes, more out of nervousness than need. "A female soldier from your regiment was found dead near her village home two days ago."

"Private Kate Nilsson." He nodded. "Devastating news for the regiment. She was a very good soldier. Served her country well in Afghanistan."

"She was murdered."

"Have you any idea by whom?" His eyes narrowed.

"Not yet." Yvonne shook her head. "But we have reason to suspect it may have been someone from this regiment."

If she had expected surprise, or any reaction at all, she would have been disappointed. His expression remained static. "What makes you say that? She was on home leave, as I understand it?" He cocked his head to one side.

"All indications suggest she was assassinated by someone of equal or better fitness. A fellow soldier."

Forster snorted. "There are fit people *outside* of the army as well, Inspector Giles."

"Ballistics have been examining the bullets. Early indications are that a Nineteen-nineties issue, Serbian pistol was used. A Zastava EZ9 is suspected. I understand your regiment served in Bosnia."

"Hang on, you think someone in my regiment smuggled in a pistol from Bosnia, back in the nineties, and used it two days ago to dispatch another of my soldiers?"

Yvonne sighed, shrugging. "We can't say when it was smuggled in, but that is one scenario. Yes, sir."

The colonel shook his head. "We take weapon smuggling seriously. I doubt-"

"Are you saying it *doesn't* happen?"

Forster's eyes strayed to the back of the room. The DI followed his gaze and saw that the aide was back, standing by the door. "Just came to ask if you'd like some tea, sir," he said, clicking his heals.

Yvonne was surprised she hadn't heard him knock.

The colonel looked from Yvonne to Dewi, who nodded.

"Yes, we will, Staff-Sergeant Jones, thank you."

"There's something else." It was Yvonne's turn to look coolly at Brod Forster. "We believe Kate was conducting an unofficial investigation into irregular deaths at this base. Including alleged suicides."

"Alleged?"

She couldn't work him out. His face was still passive. Unreadable. She could feel anxiety welling in her chest and suppressed an urge to put a hand on her heart. She had the overwhelming feeling that this man could read her far better than she could him. "Kate felt there was more to the deaths."

The colonel sighed. "When people die violent deaths, soldiers included, there are always doubts in the minds of their friends and family. It's hard for anyone to accept that a loved one could take their own life."

"Kate was a fellow soldier."

"Private Nilsson was also the dead soldiers' friend." He was back to impassive.

The DI forced her face muscles to relax. "Would it be possible to see her barrack room, please?'

"Of course." Forster nodded. "And please, do what you

need to do. I'll see to it that those you need to speak to are available to you. If not now, due to leave, then as soon as possible after Christmas."

Yvonne's eyes widened. This seemed a little easier than she'd expected. "Thank you, Brod." It felt strange using his first name.

"One more thing..." He stood up behind his desk. "As there are suspicions regarding members of my regiment, I will notify the military police. Someone will be assigned to work with you. I trust that is okay?"

Yvonne nodded, secretly hoping that whoever it was, their intention would be to help and not hinder the investigation.

As she left the colonel's office accompanied by Dewi, she breathed as though she'd spent an age under water.

THE AIDE, Staff-Sergeant Jones, accompanied them to the barrack block in which Kate Nilsson's room was located. He assured them the room had been untouched, aside from the cleaner having vacuumed the day before.

They were met at the entrance by a tall, forty-something NCO, introduced by Sergeant Jones as Platoon Sergeant Callaghan. The two officers saluted each other, the older man standing to his full height. Yvonne estimated this to be a good foot taller than she was.

Staff-Sergeant Jones left, presumably to rejoin Colonel Forster.

Sergeant Callaghan held out an arm indicating the direction he wished them to follow. "Please," he said, his voice deep and gravelly.

His gait was stiff and upright. His boots click-clacked

down the corridor. They followed him until he paused outside room eleven.

He took keys from his pocket. Shrewd, amber eyes gave them the once-over, while he unlocked the door. He stepped back, to allow Dewi to push the door open.

"I'm sorry." Dewi grimaced. "I need the men's room. Can you direct me to the toilets?"

"Sure." Callaghan looked as though he was about to verbally direct Dewi but thought better of it. "This way," he said gruffly, and the two of them continued down the corridor.

The DI found herself alone in Kate Nilsson's room. Opposite her was a large window, open a couple of inches at the top. The bed below was neatly made, the duvet a pale lavender. Dark-green, army crates were tucked underneath the bed as extra storage. To her right was shelving, covering almost the whole wall. It contained trophies, photographs, books and a framed certificate.

A large television stood on the diagonal between the window and the shelving. Behind Kate's bed were a few more shelves, photographs, folded clothes, and a small, bed-side cabinet.

It was neat and it was tidy. A feminine touch was provided by a fragrance bottle and jewellery box on top of the cabinet. Little things which were, no doubt, invaluable on those occasional nights out on the town. Yvonne took out her mobile phone and took photographs of the room, rotating her view slowly from left to right.

She heard a click-clack click-clack approaching down the corridor, stopping right outside the door. She held her breath, expecting someone to enter, her heart racing. Whoever it was continued walking after a second or two.

Yvonne exhaled loudly, curious about who had wanted to enter, but not enough to risk them coming back.

She finished taking photographs as Dewi returned. He peered around the door before coming in. The DI smiled warmly at him, letting out a deep breath.

"They don't have much, do they?" he stated, taking a quick look around. "Not much to show for their lives."

"I guess they need to travel light." Yvonne nodded. "A lot of her belongings were at her parents house. There's some stuff stored in boxes under the bed."

Dewi wandered over to the photographs, many of them taken in what appeared to be Afghanistan. One was annotated 'Bastion', which Yvonne assumed was Camp Bastion.

"I've taken photos of the layout, Dewi."

"Ma'am?" Dewi raised an eyebrow.

"Kate took a lot of photos of this room, remember?"

Dewi nodded, but looked puzzled.

"Repeatedly photographing her own room over weeks, if not months. Like she was expecting something to happen or change."

"Or like she was *worried* something might happen." Dewi nodded.

"Exactly." Yvonne knelt next to the bed and began pulling at the crates. "Like she needed to know if anyone had been in here. If anyone had touched or moved anything. If anyone had been in looking for something."

"I wouldn't do that, ma'am." Dewi pointed to the boxes. "We'd better obtain permission first."

Yvonne paused, then pushed back the crates, standing up to agree with him. "Yes. Yes, you're right, Dewi." She was just in time. Sergeant Callaghan was back. He gave a brief knock and entered. "I came to ask you if you have any questions." His gravelly voice filled the small room.

The DI put a hand on the cupboard. "We do, actually. Is there somewhere we can go?"

She was glad of the opportunity to leave. She didn't want Sergeant Callaghan observing their exploration of Kate's room.

CALLAGHAN TOOK them to the NCO's mess, picking up bottles of sparkling water from the bar, and showing Yvonne and Dewi to large chesterfields at one end of the room. The DI's eyes were drawn to a graffiti-strewn piece of wall, standing as a showpiece.

"Part of the Berlin Wall." Callaghan had returned, handing out drinks from the tray he was carrying.

"Ah, I see." Yvonne paused, genuinely impressed. "Wow."

"Our regiment was stationed in Germany for some time. That piece was bought back when we were still the Welch Fusiliers. That was before we were combined with the Royal Regiment of Wales."

"I see." Yvonne accepted the drink and took several mouthfuls. She hadn't realised how thirsty she was. She eyed the Christmas touches around the mess. They were the only souls there, aside from the guy who had come over to open the bar for the few members still at the barracks.

"I assume most of the men and women are on home leave?' She spoke her thoughts aloud, resting back on the Chesterfield and taking another sip of the water.

"We have a few here for guard purposes but, for the most part, everyone is at home. We'll take our leave when the others return."

"What are you guarding?" The DI asked innocently.

"Well, the barracks, obviously; the regimental silver, the vehicles and the ordnance." He looked taken aback that she had even asked the question.

"Sorry." She blushed. "I'm showing my total lack of knowledge of army life."

"No problem." He grinned at her.

"What about time out?" It was Dewi's turn to ask a question. "Do you get out of here for nights on the town?"

"Yes, we do. We just arrange it between the few of us that are left. It's no biggie."

Yvonne turned her gaze toward the bar, the large glass doors, and the window to the left of it. "Kate Nilsson was killed near her family home in Llydiart. It's not far from Lake Vernwy. Can I ask if anyone else from the regiment is, or was, on leave in that area of Wales?"

"Off the top of my head, I don't know. I'd have to jog my memory with the list of addresses. Would you like me to do that?"

"Please."

"How many soldiers are you in charge of, Sergeant Callaghan?"

"You can call me Pete, if you want." Sergeant Callaghan took several swigs of his water. "I've got thirty-three under my direct command." He grimaced. "Well...thirty-two now." Callaghan stretched his legs out in front of him.

"When did you last see Kate?"

"Err, let's see now, that would have been about the twentieth of December."

"And where was that?"

"The very last time?"

"Yes."

"Here. Right here in this bar. A few of us NCOs were in here, as it was the last time we would all be together before

Christmas. The beers were going down-range nicely. It was getting pretty rowdy. Kate popped over to the doors to get my attention."

"She didn't come in?"

"Well, the troops don't usually come into the officers' mess. Same as we wouldn't go into the commissioned officers' mess."

"I see. What did she want?"

"To remind me that she was off the following morning and to wish us happy Christmas."

He was pretty matter-of-fact about it. Maybe too matter-of-fact. Yvonne could see in his eyes that he knew she was analysing him.

He remained cool. "We will all miss her," he said, finally. "She was fun, and she was a damned good soldier. She'd come under fire from the ten-dollar Taliban a couple of times in Helmand and handled it better than some of the lads. She was a confident kid."

Yvonne took another few sips of her drink. "Did anyone in the regiment have an issue with Kate?"

"With Kate? No..." He paused, mouth half open. He closed it again without saying anything further. He just shook his head.

Yvonne leaned forward. "You don't seem terribly sure."

Callaghan shifted in his seat. "She was generally very popular. Though, there was one incident recently."

Dewi reopened his notebook and Yvonne's eyes narrowed.

"What incident?" The DI held her breath.

"I saw her arguing with another private. Guy from another platoon."

"When was this?"

"About a week ago."

"Who was the other private?"

"I wasn't that close to them, and he had his back to me, but I believe it was Billy Rawlins."

"What was the nature of the argument?"

"I don't know. I saw him backing off and Kate was closing the distance between them. She was quite animated. Billy was pushing her back and waving his arms, as though to say 'Leave me alone.'"

"I think we need to speak to Billy Rawlins." Yvonne pursed her lips. "Is he on home leave?"

"I would have thought so. His platoon sergeant is still on the base, so I can check in with him and find out for you, if you like."

"Yes. That would be good. Thank you."

Yvonne could tell she had gotten as much as she was going to get from Sergeant Callaghan. As soon as they finished their drinks, she made their excuses and they left.

6

DCI AND THE MILITARY POLICE

I t felt like a long and tiring journey home in the dark. Dewi drove whilst Yvonne mulled things over. The approaching car lights fuzzed into a blurry haze. The tears in her eyes, from repeated yawning, didn't help. It was only five o'clock but it felt like midnight.

"Penny for them?" Dewi turned his head briefly to her.

"I'm dying to get my hands on those boxes under Kate's bed."

"If there was anything of interest in them, ma'am, I've a feeling it'll be long gone by now."

"If the murderer had access to her room, you may be right. We need to find out who has keys and access." Yvonne pursed her lips and gazed out the window on her side. "Still, she was a bright girl with an investigative journalist as a father. She was cautious. I'll bet she found a way to leave clues somewhere in that room. Otherwise, why take all the photos? I think she was using the photos to check whether stuff had been disturbed."

"I'm guessing we'll be going back to Chester again then?" Dewi grinned.

"More than once, if I have my way." She gave a knowing smile.

"Coffee?" Dewi asked, as he swung into the Newtown station carpark.

"I'd better, or I'll be asleep at the wheel on the way home."

As they climbed the stairs, DC Clayton almost bumped into them. He was running down while putting his coat on to go home. "DCI's waiting for you, ma'am." He didn't wait for her to reply, taking the steps two at a time till the doors clanged shut at the bottom.

"Great." Yvonne sighed. "Let's sneak that coffee in first, Dewi. I've got a feeling we'll need to be awake for this one."

"I'm on it."

The DCI found them gulping next to the kettle. "Ah, there you are. I've been waiting for you to get back." He ran a hand through his hair. "I've got two officers from the Royal Military Police, Special Investigations Branch, in my office. A Warrant Officer Thornton and a Sergeant Simmonds. They want to work with you on the investigation."

Yvonne pulled a face which the DCI ignored. "Apparently, they were involved in the original investigation into two of the deaths at Dale Barracks."

The DI was awake now. Her eyes narrowed. She took a mouthful of coffee, swallowing it slowly. "They were the ones who concluded they were suicides?" Her face betrayed her gut-felt mistrust.

"Pretty much, yes." The DCI sighed. "Look, like I said, you're going to have to work *with* them, if you want to continue investigating *inside* Dale. Otherwise, you'll only be able to work on Kate Nilsson's case. You won't be able to dig any deeper. Just give them a chance." He placed his hands in his pockets. "Give them fresh insight and, who knows, their help could be invaluable. Did you find out anything at the barracks, today?"

'Bits and pieces. All about Kate, though, not about anyone else. We need to go back. Probably more than once."

"all right. Well, as I say, try to work *with* these fellows from the RMP. Extra heads and legs can only be a good thing." Christopher Llewellyn left them to the rest of their coffee.

Yvonne scowled. "They got here fast, didn't they?"

"Better go and meet them then, eh?" Dewi finished his coffee and grabbed his jacket from the back of his chair.

"Guess so." Yvonne's face relaxed a little. Perhaps she ought to give them the benefit of the doubt.

THE DCI LOOKED at his watch, as they pushed open the door. He appeared tired and impatient.

The taller of the two RMP officers introduced himself as Harry Thornton. Greying, sandy hair and a sharp, dark brown suit, he had the look of a man expecting everything to be in its place.

The shorter of the two men was almost equally dapper. Charcoal-grey suit, dark hair and very shiny shoes. He reeked of aftershave and, after they had greeted, so did Yvonne's hand.

"Sergeant Richard Simmonds," he introduced himself.

She eyed him coolly. "I understand you'd like to help us solve the murder of Kate Nilsson."

Harry Thornton cleared his throat. "I understand *you're* wanting to poke around the barracks." His gaze was equally cool.

Dewi adjusted his tie and placed his hands on his hips. "Kate Nilsson was assassinated with a weapon smuggled in from Bosnia."

"So, what are you saying?" Harry frowned.

Yvonne leaned back against the desk. "We think the weapon may have been smuggled in by someone from the regiment, during the Bosnian conflict."

"Weapons are smuggled in from Bosnia all the time. The internet makes anything possible, especially since the introduction of the dark web and bitcoin." Thornton looked at the DCI.

"The regiment was in Bosnia in the nineties." Yvonne wasn't giving up. "The pistol used to kill Kate was a nineties model."

"Even so." Thornton's gaze was back on her, challenging her to argue further.

She didn't. She was too tired. She had the feeling these two were going to make things much more difficult than they needed to be. "Will that be all, sir?" She directed the last at Christopher Llewellyn, who nodded.

"I'll let you liaise with Harry and Richard." He turned to Thornton and Simmonds. "We have your details?"

They nodded and handed cards to Yvonne and Dewi. Simmond's hand lingered on the card he gave to the DI, his twinkling eyes attempting to hold her gaze.

She made a point of looking down at the card, pulling it out of his hand and placing it in her pocket.

. . .

THAT EVENING, she telephoned her sister and spoke to the children and her mother. She wished them merry Christmas, promising she would get back down in the next few days. She was more than aware that her mother would be returning to Australia in two weeks.

Following their chat, she showered, made herself a hot chocolate, and went straight to bed. She dreamed she was taking lots of photographs of her kitchen, and the military were banging on her front door. She woke up several times, heart racing, sweat soaking her hair.

It was nearly three am before she finally fell into a deep sleep, which lasted until her alarm went off.

THE FOLLOWING DAY, Yvonne and Dewi set about finding out as much as they could about the deaths at Dale Barracks. Mostly from press reports. They had requested the files from Cheshire police but that process was still bogged down in red tape. A few phone calls gave them some information, but it was clear that Cheshire did not think it necessary to reopen the cases. Regardless, Yvonne stuck to her guns. She needed those files.

The first death had been that of Kevin McEwan, or 'Scotty'. Dewi summarised the news report for her. "Kevin 'Scotty' McEwan was found hanging from a tree on the boundary at Dale. His blood alcohol measurements showed him to be five times over the legal limit for driving, and yet he had somehow managed to climb up to a twenty-foot-high branch." Dewi ran his finger along the next line. "Friends who found him, stated they had seen tyre tracks, footprints, and what looked like the imprints of a ladder. These had supposedly gone by the time investigators got there. The site had become boggy with water. It had been raining, though an anonymous source close to Scotty had stated that the light drizzle could not have accounted for the soaking the ground appeared to have received." Dewi looked up at Yvonne. She was deep in thought.

"Surely, there was enough there to warrant a thorough investigation." She leaned back, hand on her chin. "Right, who else have we got?" She read out the next one, herself.

"Private Helen Reynolds died from heat exhaustion whilst doing heavy exercise in the gym hall. Her temperature had risen to forty-two degrees by the time she was rushed to hospital. An anonymous source, close to Helen, stated she had been carrying out prescribed physical punishment when she collapsed. This was denied by official sources."

"How old were these two?" Dewi twisted his head to scan through the article.

"Kevin McEwan was nineteen. Helen Reynolds was... eighteen. Just turned eighteen. The alleged physical punishment was known as beasting," she finished. "Oh my god."

"There's one more which stands out." Dewi examined the last article. "Thomas Rendon, aged twenty. He allegedly shot himself after suffering depression. He'd sustained two bullets to the chest and one to the head. When asked, the MOD stated that the automatic rifle had carried on firing as he fell to the ground, explaining the number of wounds."

"Really?" The DI appeared sceptical.

"Automatics do get off several rounds very quickly, ma'am." Dewi tapped his pen on the desk. "I'll google for more info. See what's out there until we can get those files from Cheshire."

"We can speak to Lars Nilsson again, too. I'm sure there's more he's not saying. If he encouraged his daughter to look into those deaths, I'll bet he was expecting her to keep feeding back to him."

"Didn't you say you thought his wife looked scared, too?" Dewi asked, hands deep in pockets.

"Yes. I wonder how much she knows." The DI put her pen down. "One thing's for sure, we're unlikely to get anything from Hayley Nilsson. At least, not yet."

"So, what's the next step, then? Back to Dale?" Dewi got up from his chair.

"We talk to the ordinary soldiers. The friends of Kate and the others. Find out what they know."

"If they'll talk to us."

"We've got to hope they'll at least give us something." She sighed. "Before that, we go back to Lars Nilsson and find out the identity of Kate's closest friend at the barracks."

"I'll give him a call. Set it up." Dewi set off down the corridor, leaving Yvonne to write her 'to do' list. It was drizzling outside. She stared out at the grey sky, watching the rivulets wend their way down the pane. The last snow on the ground was fast disappearing. So much for Christmas.

LARS NILSSON'S eyes flicked from side-to-side. "Kate had a number of friends at the barracks-"

Yvonne was losing patience. "Mr. Nilsson, either you wish your daughter's murder solved or you don't. We're currently working in the dark. The leads are all at that barracks. We have to start somewhere...with someone."

Lars looked pained.

The DI relented. "Look, I know you're grieving the loss of your daughter. She was a good and courageous young woman. I just need to know who she might have confided in at the base. If you know something, and you want us to catch your daughter's killer, please help us."

Lars ran a hand through his hair. His eyes were rimmed with red and they glistened with tears, barely held back. "Don't doubt that I loved my daughter. My concern now is for her best friend. She didn't want him dragged into it. She begged me not to mention him, if anything happened to her."

The DI's gaze was soft. "Lars, he's probably already in danger. His best hope may be us finding the killer or killers. Whoever killed Kate will be wanting to cover all tracks. Remove all traces of any information she had uncovered. Kate's best friend may already be in the firing line. Sorry... no pun intended."

Lars picked up a photograph of Kate from the mantlepiece and stared softly at it. "His name is Wayne Hedges. Private Wayne Hedges."

"Do you have a home address for him?"

"Home?" Lars raised an eyebrow.

"Well, I'm guessing he'll be on home leave right now, and that may be the safest place to talk to him."

"Err...yes, we should have that. We'll need to go up to Kate's room. There are some letters in her top drawer. There are several from Wayne."

It was Yvonne's turn to raise an eyebrow.

"Well, doesn't every father keep a check on their daughter's activities?"

"I guess so."

"His home address should be on them."

Yvonne smiled and nodded her thank you. Lars Nilsson had redeemed himself.

. . .

Armed with an address, she rejoined Dewi at the car. "Got it." Her eyes shone. "Let's go there now and speak to him, before he heads back to the base."

"I take it we're not taking Dick and Harry." Dewi grinned at his own cheeky reference to Simmonds and Thornton.

"No, the SOBs, err... I mean SIBs," Yvonne grinned back, "are to be kept in the dark about this one. They can join us when we go to Dale."

"Roger that." Dewi laughed out loud.

"Do you mind staying in the car again?" Yvonne smiled apologetically at Dewi, placing a hand on his arm.

"What, again?" Dewi wore a hurt look which she suspected was purely for effect. He sniffed under each of his arms. "Is it B.O.?"

She smacked him lightly on the shoulder. "Behave. You know full-well I'd tell you if you'd suddenly developed a problem with personal hygiene. I just want to dip a toe in the water. Get the lie of the land. If Private Hedges is running scared, he might balk at two detectives turning up at his door."

"Don't worry, ma'am," Dewi smiled. "I get it. I'll wait here. You could have told me earlier, though. I'd have brought some donuts."

"Dewi, we're not in America." She laughed as she left the car but it was short-lived. She was already mentally rehearsing what she wanted to ask Wayne.

The address in Merthyr Tydfil, in Mid-Glamorgan, was a tiny, terraced house in a long street of the same. Built as miners' cottages, there were many of them in the valleys of South Wales.

The area carried the dubious title of one of Europe's poorest regions. Dewi had explained that the people would argue it was also one of Europe's most friendly. That the people there would give you their last, if they thought you were hungry. The Merthyr coat of arms on the town's welcome sign would surely support that. It read, 'Nad cadarn ond brodyrdde'. Dewi had translated that as, 'Only brotherhood is strong'.

The DI was hoping that Wayne would give her Kate Nilsson's last thoughts.

SHE TOOK a moment to gather her thoughts, then knocked twice on the door.

Feet pounded down the stairs and the door was opened by a young man in his mid-to-late twenties, wearing only a pair of jeans. Both his feet and his torso were bare. His blonde hair was closely cropped to his head. His striking blue eyes peered questioningly at her.

"DI Giles," she introduced herself, flashing her warrant card. "I'm looking for Wayne Hedges."

The young man's face darkened. "Why? What's he done?" He peered around her, as though expecting to see more officers or a marked vehicle.

"He hasn't done anything," she reassured, guessing this must be Wayne. "I just want to talk to him about his friend, Kate Nilsson."

The young man stepped back, attempting to close the door. The DI put her foot in, and winced at the pain. "Please, I want to help."

He opened the door again, staring at her foot. "Help with what?"

"You do know Kate was murdered?"

He paled and opened his mouth, as though to say something, but shut it again. He shook his head.

"I'm so sorry, Wayne. I thought you would have known. It's been all over the news."

"I didn't tell you I was Wayne." His tone was sullen.

"You didn't need to." Her gaze was soft. "May I come in? Is anyone else home?"

"No. My parents have gone around to friends." He was frowning, as though trying to digest what he had just heard. "You said Kate was murdered. When? Who?"

"Several days ago. We're still trying to establish who."

He stepped back to allow her into the hallway.

She continued. "We thought you might be able to help us-"

"You alone?" Once more, he furtively glanced around the street outside.

"No. My DS is in the car."

"I didn't see any car."

"It's unmarked."

"Good." He had the appearance of someone who did not know what to do or think next.

"Can I make you a cup of tea?" she asked. "Where's the best place to talk?"

He nodded and led the way to the kitchen, through the narrow hallway.

A small table and three chairs, stood to one side of the small, square kitchen. Wayne filled a whistle kettle and placed it on the gas hob, which he lit with a match after several attempts with the knob. Several dead matches lay strewn around the countertop.

"How long had you known Kate?" She pulled out her notebook.

"We met at the start of our basic training. What happened to her?" His eyes pierced her. "How did she die?"

"She was shot, Wayne. Several times, with a pistol."

He turned away. "Where?"

"Not far from her home in Llydiart."

He was staring out of the kitchen window. The kettle whistled low and soft, moving to a harsh noise as the DI jumped up to rescue it from the hob. Wayne appeared not to notice.

"We were seventeen. That was eight years ago. She said she liked me because I treated her like a person and not a piece of meat."

"Who treated her like a piece of meat?"

"Other recruits. Some of the officers."

"NCOs?"

"Yeah. One NCO in particular."

"Who was that?" Yvonne's delivery was gentle.

Wayne had fallen silent.

"Wayne?" She poured water onto the teabags. Steam curled up. She watched the myriad tiny droplets in it, waiting for him to answer.

"Sergeant Callaghan."

"Sergeant Callaghan-"

"She said he'd come onto her so many times. Didn't want to take no for answer. She wasn't that sort of a girl, you know?"

"And what sort of a girl was that?"

"The sort who uses her looks to get favours outta the officers and the lads. She was just like the rest of us. One of the lads, almost. She'd showed the Talies on a few occasion."

"The Talies?"

"The Taliban."

"That was in Afghanistan, right?"

"Yeah. 'Course. She was a good shot and a good soldier. She was a fantastic friend."

Yvonne saw the drips falling into the sink. He was still looking through the window.

"How did she deal with Sergeant Callaghan?"

"Avoided him whenever she could. When she did have to deal with him, she kept it to a minimum. He'd punish her for the least little thing. Have her running round the parade ground at midnight."

"Did he only do that to Kate?"

"No. To be fair, he was pretty harsh with the lads, as well. He just seemed to be particularly harsh with Kate."

"Did any of the other officers know what was happening?"

"Some of them, definitely. Others? I don't know."

"Did the major-general know?"

"What, ole Broddy Forster?"

"Yes."

"No. He didn't know. Head in the clouds. Ole Broddy thinks the regiment runs like a well-oiled machine. He's a good sort, he is. His heart's in the right place. None of the officers put a foot out of line when he's around."

"Well, that's something. What about the other officers?"

"Some of them, straight as an arrow. Others..." He finally turned to face her. "You'd see them getting pissed-up in the mess. Pints going down-range like there's no tomorrow. Be in there all night sometimes. Stumble out when it was light the next morning."

"Were they disciplined?"

"If Forster heard about it, yeah."

"How did this affect Kate?"

"Well, she reckoned a few times they'd been banging on her door in the small hours, begging to be let in."

"Did she let them in?"

"No. No." He gave her a hard look. "I told you, she wasn't that sort of girl."

"What did they do when she refused to let them in?"

"Well, they'd give up, eventually. Go back to their rooms and crawl into bed. She reckoned one or two of them had tried walking in on her when she was having a shower."

"Was she scared?"

"Not really. They tended to give up without forcing it."

"Did any other females go through this?"

"We only have a few girls in the regiment, and yeah, I think all of them have had the same thing, and not just from the officers. A few of the lads as well. When they've got a few beers inside them. Thankfully, most of the lads do their drinking in Chester and not on the base."

"No wonder she thought you were a breath of fresh air." Yvonne handed Wayne his mug, which he accepted with a sad smile.

"She and her family were afraid of something. Can you tell me what that was?"

"No." He said it a little too quickly.

"Kate was investigating something, wasn't she?" The DI held her breath.

Wayne stiffened. "Was she?" he asked, eventually.

"There have been other deaths in strange or suspicious circumstances. Deaths at the base. Kate was looking into them. Unofficially."

"I wouldn't know about that."

"About the deaths? Or about Kate's looking into them?"

"About anything." He downed his tea in one.

"You mean you won't talk to me about it."

He shook his head.

Yvonne gave him her card. "Please call me if you change your mind."

"What will I do without her, miss?" He asked the question almost like a schoolboy might ask his teacher.

"Stay safe. Until we catch Kate's killer, I recommend you not go anywhere alone."

"Even on the base?"

"Perhaps especially on the base. Stay with people you can trust. And if you change your mind, call me. Information you may have could help to catch Kate's killer. The sooner the killer or killers are caught, the better for everyone. Yourself included."

Wayne nodded and walked with the DI to see her out.

"When are your parents back?" she asked.

"Anytime soon," he answered, while holding the door open for her.

"Remember to call me if you need to talk, Wayne."

"Yes, miss."

"Did you get anything?" Dewi asked, as she climbed back into the car.

"I did, actually. Not everything I wanted, but he gave me something to work with. We'll get clearance from the DCI and re-visit Dale."

"What about Dick and Harry?"

Yvonne pulled a face. "You may have to keep them occupied while I do a bit of digging. Think you can manage it?"

Dewi's answer was a big grin.

She turned to stare into the distance. "Before we go back to Dale, I'd like to talk to Kevin McEwan's parents. His death was the first, in 2009. His mum and dad may give us more names. They may even have suspicions about who was involved."

"Okay."

"I don't want anyone at the barracks to know we're looking into other deaths in any serious way. Let them think we're only interested in Kate's death. That should make it a little less dangerous for the deceased's friends."

"I'm with you."

"I've managed to find Mr and Mrs McEwan, from the inquest records. We're going there to talk to them."

"Right."

"We don't need to go too far. They live in Builth Wells. They've been trying to get their son's case reopened."

"Let's do it."

7

SCOTTY'S PARENTS

The drive to Builth took them on windy back-roads, through Dolfor, Llanbadarn Fynydd and Llandrindod Wells, going south. Builth lay on the Brecon road. A place of rolling hills on the edge of the Brecon Beacons. They followed the road over the stone bridge and round to the right. Dewi studied the street map while Yvonne followed the sat nav. The DI smiled at this old-fashioned quirk in her DS. She quite liked it.

They found the black-and-white, semi-detached house with relative ease. They stood side-by-side, as the DI rang the door bell.

Gordon McEwan opened the door, dressed casually and wearing slippers. He'd been expecting them, since Dewi had phoned earlier. He welcomed them in and called to his wife, Victoria. Rich smells of stew or casserole wafted through the house, teasing the two detectives' stomachs.

They removed their shoes, and Gordon showed them through to a medium-sized lounge. They sat on a floral-patterned sofa and saw photographs of Scotty in his uniform, on the sideboards and mantelpiece.

Yvonne took out her notebook. "Thank you for seeing us, Mr and Mrs McEwan."

"Please call us Gordon and Vicky." Gordon's smile was stiff, though his eyes betrayed an intense interest. "We're so glad you're reopening the case into our son's death. We've been waiting so long."

The DI and Dewi exchanged glances.

Dewi cleared his throat. "Gordon, we have to tell you this is not an official reopening of Kevin's case. We're investigating the death of another soldier, killed just before Christmas. Private Kate Nilsson. Same regiment as Kevin."

"Then why?" The couple appeared confused, their excitement dissipating in sighs.

"It's possible there's a connection. We would ask you to keep that to yourselves for the moment, lives may depend on it."

Gordon perched on the end of his chair, elbows on his knees, hands clasped.

Dewi continued. "We believe Kate Nilsson was conducting an unofficial investigation into your son's death, and the deaths of other young soldiers, when she was killed. Obviously, we don't yet know if she was killed for that reason, but it's a possibility." Dewi stopped, looking towards the DI.

Yvonne turned her gaze from Gordon to Vicky and back. "Tell us about Kevin. He was known as Scotty, wasn't he? What was he like? Was he happy in the army?"

"Scotty was an orphan. His real parents were killed, when he was only five, in a road traffic collision. He spent most of his formative years in and out of care homes. He'd had some brushes with the law and could be a bit wild. We adopted him when he was thirteen, after a year of being his foster carers."

"Where was he from, originally?"

"Wrexham, his family were from. He was at a care home there between the ages of seven and eleven. Sunnymede, I think it was called."

"Sunnymede," Yvonne repeated, getting everything down in her pocketbook. "When did he make the decision to join the army?"

Vicky took over the telling. "He was fifteen when he first talked about the army. Several of his friends had either joined or were thinking of joining. There'd been a series of adverts on the telly which drew them in. For kids like Kevin, it was a way of belonging after spending so long feeling like an outsider."

Yvonne nodded. "I can see how that might be the case. But you'd given him a loving home. Did he not feel like he belonged with you?"

"He did." Gordon brushed his trouser legs with his hand. "But children who spend so long in care can become institutionalised, almost. They are used to more going on. I think he was bored a lot of the time. Always craving excitement. To us, the army represented a chance for him to straighten out and see the world. Have structure and discipline in his life. And, of course, he would then progress to have a career outside of the army, using the skills he'd acquired along the way."

Yvonne pursed her lips. "You certainly couldn't have foreseen what happened to him."

"No. We didn't see that coming. Not in a million years."

"The army investigation concluded that your son had taken his own life. Was he depressed?"

Gordon shook his head, exasperation creeping into his voice. "Look, Scotty had his ups and downs like all teenagers. But he wasn't suicidal. Hell, he'd told us about a lass he'd met only a couple of weeks before he died. He was excited. He'd been back to Wrexham for a party with some of his old friends. He'd been on a high. We spoke to him three days before he died. He said he was happy and that things were really coming together. He liked the regiment. Took pride in its history. He was looking forward to serving in Afghanistan." Gordon looked down at his shoes. "He never got the chance."

"They said he'd been drinking the night of his death," Yvonne said, gently. "Do you think that might have impacted on his emotions?"

Victoria levelled her gaze at the DI. "His friends said, when they found him, there were indications that others had been there."

"I read about that." Yvonne nodded. "But if there were any traces, they were gone when investigators got there."

"Yes, because someone saturated the ground. Who was it that destroyed all the evidence?"

"You don't believe it was the rain?"

"No. No, we don't believe it was the bloody rain." Gordon sent saliva projectiles out over the carpet. "A light drizzle does not do that. Someone turned the hoses on it. Someone wiped all traces."

"Who found your son, Gordon?" The DI's voice remained calm and soft.

"Tom. Tom Rendon and a chap called Stephen Whyte."

"Tom Rendon? *The* Tom Rendon who was also alleged to have committed suicide?"

"That's the one." Gordon bought both palms down on his knees with an emphatic slap.

"I see." The DI, still scribbling madly, frowned. "What about this Stephen Whyte? Is he still with the regiment?"

"Yes. I believe he's a corporal, now."

"Corporal Stephen Whyte. I think we'll be talking to him as soon as we can."

"Be careful." Gordon's eyes were earnest, as he flicked his gaze between Yvonne and Dewi. "There are powerful people at work. People who do not want the cases reopened. God knows, we've hit enough brick walls to know. *And* received anonymous letters warning us off."

"Do you still have the letters?"

"No. I burned them." Gordon stood, hands on hips. "Whoever these people are, they'll do anything to prevent the truth coming out. Anything."

ON THE WAY back to Newtown, Yvonne was pensive.

Dewi yawned. "You gonna find Stephen Whyte first?"

"If I can. The difficulty is knowing where to start. I think we need Jones and Clayton to do a bit of digging. We need to be careful, Dewi."

"Ma'am?"

"We've been narrowing our focus. That's dangerous. Let's widen it again. Find out if Kate had boyfriends, dates or liaisons. Find out what else she was into. Just because she was investigating suspicious deaths doesn't mean that was why she was killed. We mustn't miss anything."

"This is a good lead, though."

"It certainly is, Dewi. It certainly is."

YVONNE PUNCHED the numbers into her mobile and waited, holding her breath. If she didn't get him now, he'd be back at the base, and setting things up would be that much more difficult.

A gruff, older voice answered. "Ron Hedges."

"Oh, er, hello. I was looking for Wayne Hedges. Could I speak to him, please?"

"Who's calling?"

"You can tell him it's Yvonne. We spoke the other day. He'll know who I am."

"I'll go see if he's available."

She could hear the TV in the background. The sound of voices, of feet pounding down the stairs.

"Wayne Hedges."

"Hi, Wayne. It's DI Giles. We spoke the other day."

"I know. What's the matter?" he said, his tone clipped.

"Nothing's the matter, Wayne. I wanted to ask a favour. I need your help."

"Oh." He sounded disappointed.

"It could help me solve your friend's murder," she added.

"What d'you want me to do?"

Yvonne bit her lip. "Wayne, I think it's important I speak to Stephen Whyte. Do you know him?"

There was a pause, then, "I know of him. I don't know him that well. I've seen him around. You mean Corporal Whyte?"

"Yes. Corporal Whyte. Can you set it up? Can you ask him if he'll meet me? Tell him he can choose the place and time. I'll be there."

"What shall I say it's about?"

She sensed a reluctance, but pressed on. "Tell him it's to talk about his friends Scotty McEwan and Tom Rendon." There was silence on the other end of the line. "Wayne?"

"What if he won't speak to you?"

"I'll cross that line when I come to it. Please tell him it is very, *very* important. And, Wayne?"

"Yes?"

"Please don't tell anyone else about the meeting. Ask Stephen to keep it to himself. Given what happened to Kate, I don't want either of you put at risk. Is that clear?"

"I'll try."

"Good man. Wayne, do you still have my card?"

"Yes, I have it."

'Call me when you've set it up, please."

"It'll be when I get back to the base. You know I can't contact him until then."

"I know. And, remember, keep it under your hat."

"Got it." There was a click at the other end and he was gone.

SHE TOOK a couple of deep breaths and headed off to find Dewi. She found him flicking through the County Times, in the office.

"There you are." He put the paper down, his eyebrows raised.

"Sorry, I was making a phone call." She could see he wanted more. "I'm trying to set up a meeting with Stephen Whyte."

"I thought we were heading to Dale tomorrow?" Dewi frowned. "Get a look in those boxes."

"We are. I won't know, until it's arranged, when the meeting with Whyte will take place."

Dewi relaxed. "Ah, I see. Okay. Well, we'd better contact Dick and Harry. We're under strict instruction to have them with us, whenever we're at the barracks."

Yvonne pulled a face but giggled at the cheeky reference from her wicked sergeant.

She caught sight of the main headline in the Times, 'Heinous Murder of Kate Nilsson. Still no leads', and sighed. "Right, Dewi, get Dick and Harry on the blower and let's get to Chester."

"Right, you are, ma'am."

8

THINGS ARE HOTTING UP

'Dick and Harry' met them as soon as they arrived at the base. Suited and booted, they made Yvonne feel dog-eared and jaded. She shook hands with them, as Dewi caught up after parking the car. She hadn't wanted them there, but was determined to make the best of it.

Harry was frowning.

"Journey okay?" she asked, wincing at how lame that sounded.

"It was." Harry nodded. "Only one hold-up. A lot better than last time. You've been in Private Nilsson's room before?" He asked the question but appeared to already know the answer. His gaze wandered.

"Yes. Once before. Three days ago. Why?" She kept her gaze steady.

"I just wondered why the need to go through it again?" His expression stayed neutral. He wasn't giving anything away.

"Kate's storage boxes, under her bed. We didn't get a chance to go through them last time."

"You think there'll be a clue in there?"

"You're military police. What do you think?" she answered, tartly.

He looked down at his shiny shoes and the DI relented.

"I'm sorry. I didn't mean to be rude.What I meant was, I don't know, but I want no stone unturned." She could have told him about the numerous photos Kate had taken of her room, but chose not to. She still had no idea who she could trust. Dick and Harry were still regarded with suspicion.

AT FIRST GLANCE, Kate's room appeared untouched since their last visit. On further inspection, someone had shut the open window and there were one or two dead flies on the window ledge.

It was a tight squeeze, fitting all four into Kate's tiny room.

Simmonds was standing a little too close. The DI tapped Dewi on the shoulder and, when Simmonds wasn't looking, she traded places with her DS.

They donned latex gloves and pulled out the two cargo boxes from under the bed.

Old photographs, spare clothes and spare bits of kit, including a helmet and books. They examined each item, Dewi taking photographs with his mobile.

Yvonne mused that the last person to touch these things may have been Kate. She wondered what the soldier would have been thinking, as she organised her things in these boxes. Surely, not that she would be dead before Christmas. The DI shuddered. Dewi placed a hand on her arm. Perhaps he'd been thinking along similar lines.

The DI's hands were gentle - reverent- as she handled those things. It pained her to think that when they'd finished, Kate's room and belongings would smell of Dick Simmonds' aftershave.

It was then that she saw it. A yellow, manilla folder. She reached for it, only for Simmonds to beat her to it. He opened the flap and stood. The DI stood also, attempting to get a look. Simmonds moved it away from her.

"Can I see?" The question was as forceful as she could make it, without seeming overly aggressive.

Simmonds shook his head. "We'll need clearance. There's material in here with a classified stamp on it. We'll have to take this."

"Wait, we're investigating officers, we've a right to see it." Yvonne's eyes blazed, her hands firmly on her hips.

"And you will." Harry's voice was gentle. "Just as soon as we've had the okay from the MOD and senior officers."

With that, the yellow manilla folder disappeared into Simmonds leather satchel.

"How do we know it won't be tampered with?" She couldn't hide her frustration.

"You'll have to trust us," Thornton answered. "We're investigating officers, too."

The DI's mobile began bleating in her pocket. She checked the screen. "It's my sister, she apologised. "My mother is home from Australia." She gave Dewi a look and ducked out of the room. She made her way to where she'd seen Dewi go to the toilet on their previous visit.

Once inside the cubicle, she spoke in a loud whisper. "Wayne?"

"I've got good news for you."

"Go on." Her hand shook.

"Corporal Whyte has agreed to meet you tonight."

"Tonight? Where? What time?"

"St. John's Priory, in Chester. Seven o'clock. Go there alone."

"Where's-" Too late. He was gone.

Yvonne checked her watch. It was approaching one o'clock. She opened the internet on her mobile. The 4G signal was fading in and out but she managed to bring up Google maps and the Priory.

A quick read informed her that St. Johns was a half-ruinous church. A solid oak coffin was set high in the wall of the Chancel ruins. One thing was for sure, she'd know when she found it. Whether she'd be able to hold her nerve in such a place would be a different matter.

There was a knock on the cubicle door. She stuffed her mobile in her pocket.

"Ma'am?" It was Dewi.

She felt huge relief as she pushed open the door. "Fancy going into Chester for lunch?"

Dewi shrugged, looking confused. "Sure." He'd obviously been expecting to find her fuming over the lost manilla file. Truth was, she'd almost forgotten it.

SHE FILLED him in over lunch, and they walked part of Chester wall, as tourists might. They made sure they knew exactly where St. John's Priory was. The DI thought it best not to go too near, just in case they were being followed. At seven o'clock it would be dark.

DEWI PARKED the car as close as he could. It still felt a long distance to walk in the dark. The street lights provided little reassurance.

Yvonne pulled her long, wool coat tightly around her. Hands in her pockets. Several times, she thought she heard something behind, but turning, found nothing. No-one there. She stopped at a bench, holding tightly to the back of it. Anxiety washing over her like a fountain. Her muscles trembled from fear and cold.

St. Johns was ahead, lit from below, the lamps aimed at the towers. Her shaking intensified as she fought the over-whelming urge to run. Dewi had said he would be no more than ten seconds away, but she couldn't see him. So, it was little comfort.

"Over here."

She almost jumped out of her skin. Her legs refused to move.

"Over here." A silhouetted figure in a hoodie waved to her.

She wanted to run, sweat snaking down her back as she thought of Kate. Thought of that beautiful woman cut down in her prime. Face down in the mud.

She concentrated on putting one foot in front of the other, praying that Dewi really was only ten seconds away. Step by tentative step, she steeled herself on into the priory grounds. She gripped the can of mace in her pocket and made her way to the hooded figure.

"Are you Inspector Giles? Yvonne Giles?"

She couldn't see the face of the man asking the question.

"I am Yvonne Giles. Are you Corporal Whyte?" Her hand gripping the mace relaxed.

"You come alone?" He flicked his head from side-to-side. Eyes darting furtively around.

"Yes. My DS is parked a couple of streets away."

"Good. You wanted to talk to me. Here I am."

"Do you have ID on you?"

He pulled a wallet out of his pocket, pausing to ask, "Do you?"

The DI pulled out her warrant holder.

"What did you want to know?" He grabbed her and pulled her further into the shadow.

She resisted the urge to spray him in the face. "I'm investigating the murder of Kate Nilsson."

"I know. Wayne told me. It's why I'm here. I wouldn't have risked this for anyone else. Kate was a good woman. She had a good heart but she picked a battle with evil." He shook his head.

"Stephen, I understand you found Scotty McEwan, the night he hanged himself."

"I thought this was about Kate."

"It is. Do you know who killed her?"

He shook his head again. "No. I wish I did, I'd-"

"Do you have a suspicion?"

"Not one that you'd find much use, and Scotty didn't hang himself."

"What makes you so sure?"

An owl screeched overhead. The DI ducked and grabbed Stephen's arm. She let go, embarrassed.

"He was bladdered. He couldn't have done it. We'd all been drinking together. He was happy. Even if he could have done it, he wouldn't have. Are you finally looking into this properly?"

"I want to. I'm trying to. I want to know what you saw. Scotty's father said you'd seen evidence of the involvement of others in his death."

"I did. There were tyre tracks. Probably Land Rover; at least three sets of footprints, including Scotty's, and marks left from the feet of a folding ladder."

"Are you sure about that? You said you'd been drinking."

"I had. But finding your friend dead kind of sobers you up, doesn't it? Anyway," he kicked a small stone into the distance, "Tom wasn't drunk. Tom was driving. He'd had one pint."

"Tom? You mean Tom Rendon?"

"Yeah. Tom Rendon. He knew. He reported it to Callaghan and Jones. They suggested waiting till the morning, to take a look."

"What about Scotty? They left him there till morning?" She shook her head, mouth wide open.

"No. No, we cut him down. Drove him to the mess. That was my idea and it was dumb. I thought I'd felt a pulse. An ambulance was called but he'd gone." Stephen's voice choked. "Tom tried to get officers to go back to the scene but they said we were all too drunk and the scene would be examined in the morning."

"Were the police called?"

"Yes, but not until the morning."

"Wouldn't ambulance staff have called the police?"

"Well, if they did, no-one came. Police did come out, but not until the following day."

"And that's when the field was found to be waterlogged."

"Yeah."

"What about Tom? They said he shot himself."

"I know they did. A couple of years later, just after his second tour of Afghanistan. He was found with his rifle. One shot to the head and two to the chest."

"An automatic rifle."

"Yes, but if you're implying that was why so many bullets, I'd say again - Tom wasn't suicidal."

"Was it possible for him to have gotten off two more rounds as he fell?"

"Technically, maybe, but he *wasn't* depressed."

"What about PTSD. Could he have been suffering after two tours of Afghanistan?"

Stephen flicked his head left and right again. "Look, I gotta go. Start with Callaghan and Jones, and move up. Whoever washed away that evidence had power. Start there."

He was gone. Yvonne was once more alone and afraid. Footsteps behind had her reaching for her mace. She turned as the presence reached her shoulder, and sprayed Dewi, full face.

"Oh my god, Dewi!" She didn't know whether to laugh or cry.

Dewi rolled around cursing and spluttering. Yvonne took a packet of tissues from her bag and tried to mop his face. He was still stumbling around, tears streaming.

"Come on, I'll drive you to the hospital." Yvonne draped his arm over her shoulder and guided him back to the car. He was beginning to recover by the time she got him in.

At the hospital, she could tell that the staff, albeit caring, thought it hilarious that a couple of cops had been involved in an accidental macing. More than one nurse smirked when she told them what happened. This had been one hell of a long day.

THE FOLLOWING DAY, DC Clayton caught up with Yvonne whilst she was going through her mail.

"Ma'am, we've got an address for an army friend of Helen Reynolds. One Sam Walters. He was probably her closest friend at the time of her death. Looks like he left the army two years ago."

"Dai, thank you." Yvonne put down her mail and

perched on the edge of her desk. "That's a good find. Maybe you can come with me, when I go to see Sam. Where is he? And what's he doing now?"

"He lives in Llanwrtyd Wells and works in construction. He's doing some work with the teams on the Newtown bypass. Might be easier talking to him on a lunch break than hunting him down at home."

The DI nodded. "Certainly easier than driving all the way to Llanwrtyd. Okay, we'll speak to Sam, if he'll talk to us, but I really wish we could quiz the major-general about Helen's death. A soldier dying during a physical punishment is manslaughter in my book."

"Why don't you just go ahead and ask him about it?" Dai raised his eyebrows.

"I can't. At least, not yet. It would be different if Kate had found concrete evidence of wrongdoing. I'd have reason enough, right there. I could quiz the lot of them. And I could legitimately link their deaths to Kate's. Which reminds me." Yvonne ran her hands through her hair. "I want to speak to the DCI. I'd like him to put pressure on the army SIB officers to give me a folder they took from Kate's things."

"What was in the folder?" Clayton felt in his pockets for his cigarettes and pulled out a vaper.

"You quitting?" Yvonne appeared incredulous.

Clayton grinned. "Trying to. The wife's trying for our third child and putting the pressure on." He pulled a face.

The DI laughed. "Good for her. I'm glad. You were smoking too many of those death sticks." She winked. "Right, good work tracing Sam Walters. I'm off to find the DCI. Wish me luck."

. . .

SHE FOUND him pouring coffee from the machine. She thought she caught a fleeting look of disappointment. Did he know what was coming?

"Yvonne, how's things?"

"Coming along, sir. I wanted to talk to you about those two RMP officers, actually."

"Thornton and Simmonds?"

"Yes." She was glad the DCI had named them. She'd have been tempted to refer to them by Dewi's irreverent nicknames. "Yes, Thornton and Simmonds. They took a folder from Kate's room when we were going through her things."

"Want one?" Llewellyn asked, referring to the coffee he was now sipping.

"Er, yes. Go on, then. As I was saying," she sighed, "they took a manilla folder, saying it was classified material and they needed clearance from the MOD in order to sanction its handover to us."

"Well, it *is* army property, Yvonne."

"Well, yes, of course it is. But it's potentially material evidence in connection with her murder."

The DCI raised an eyebrow. "If that is the case, then I'm sure they'll get it back to you as quickly as possible."

"Yes, but probably heavily redacted. You know as well as I do that it's likely to be so heavily redacted it'll be utterly useless."

"I don't know anything of the sort. Look, those two men seem professional to me. They're police like us. They'll want to get to the truth."

"They're army." Yvonne's eyes flashed fire. "We don't know that they won't help cover up for the MOD."

"I don't think that attitude is helpful, Yvonne. What have

you got against Thornton and Simmonds?" The DCI sighed and handed her a mug.

"I think Kate may have been murdered because she was looking into suspicious deaths at the base. If I'm right, the cover-up may go all the way to the top."

Yvonne was thinking of what Corporal Whyte had said in the grounds of St Johns Priory. 'Start with Callaghan and Jones and work up'. "Sir, if there has been a cover-up, it was almost certainly orchestrated at officer level or higher. I don't think we should rely on Dick and Harry to necessarily do the right thing."

"Dick and Harry?" Llewellyn raised an eyebrow at her, again.

Yvonne coloured. She knew she'd get caught out. Damn Dewi, he always managed to get her in trouble, even when he wasn't here.

"Look," he put a hand on her shoulder, "I'll speak with Forster. See if I can get you that file back with as little redaction as possible, okay? I can't promise I'll succeed, but I'll try."

Yvonne sipped her coffee and nodded. "I'd really appreciate that, sir. Thank you." She took another sip. "You should make coffee more often, Chris. This is good." She gave him a cheeky smile and turned for the door, leaving him watching her back, as she left. He took a sip of his own coffee and savoured it. She had a point, it *was* good.

9

TASHA'S NEW HOME BY THE SEA

The sun loomed large, though the air was bitterly cold. The crisp, blue sky was peppered with the condensation trails from aircraft, as Yvonne set out on her forty-five minute journey to Aberdovey.

She drove faster than usual. Head spinning with tidbits from the case. She was angsty because of this, and because of the guilt she felt at heading to Tasha's new weekend home instead of her sister's house, to see her family. She bit her lip. She'd catch up with Kim and her mum next weekend, and *definitely* before her mum left for Australia again.

She could hear the gulls and smell the sea long before she caught sight of the bright sunlight bouncing off the surface ripples. The briny, fishy smell of childhood holidays and the less welcome, recent memories of blood-soaked crime scenes. She hadn't been out this way since hunting down the priest-slayer, and she was glad this trip was a happier occasion.

She double-checked the sat nav as she took a left towards the coast. Down a little driveway and on towards a pale-blue cottage. She knew she'd got the right place when she spotted a smiling Tasha, in oversized dungarees, wandering around the yard.

The psychologist held a paint can in one hand and a large brush in the other. A huge grin and several paint smears covered her face. "Ta-dah," she said, spreading her arms and turning round in front of her new home.

Yvonne got out of her Renault and couldn't help but smile back, running over to give her speckled friend a hug.

"What do you think?" Tasha nodded in the direction of the house.

"Well, it's in a fantastic position." Yvonne looked outwards, the sea to her right and the estuary to her left. She looked back at the house. "Is it all-wood construction?"

"Pretty much." Tasha nodded. "There's some brick at the foundation but, yeah, a lot of wood." She waved the can and brush. "And a helluva lot of painting for me."

"I can see that." Yvonne laughed. "You need a few nails and screws, as well, by the look of things."

Tasha screwed her face up. "Paint's peeling and a few things are wonky but, hey, it's got heaps of potential and loads of character. And just wait till you see the size of my lounge window. A view to die for."

Yvonne took off her shoes, as they went inside. She needn't have. There was sand and leaves scattered everywhere on the wooden floor. A broom leaned casually against the door-frame.

"Want a cuppa? Or something stronger?" Tasha asked, taking the DI's coat.

Yvonne stood in the lounge window, looking out. Almost the whole wall had been given over to the huge, sliding-door window, and the view really was gorgeous. The lounge melted into the wooden veranda and on to the beach and sea. Gulls swooped in and around the estuary and little boats glinted on the water. Winter sunlight was everywhere. Tasha's lounge was also surprisingly warm, which pleased the DI.

"Come on, I'll show you the kitchen." Tasha grabbed her friend's arm and they crossed the old, wooden floorboards, heading for the little galley kitchen. "The electrics need rewiring and there's one or two small leaks in the plumbing but, aside from that, everything works."

"I'll have a cuppa, please. If that's okay." Yvonne smiled. "I think it's lovely, and it has oodles of charm. You got anyone coming to fix the electrics and plumbing?"

Tasha filled the kettle. "Yes. Next week. That's when the plumber gets here." She pulled a face. "It's the earliest he could do. And the electrician comes the week after that."

"How long you down for, then?" Yvonne opened the tiny fridge to get the milk.

"Two weeks, initially. Then I hope to be down most weekends, and for the occasional longer holiday. To be honest, I'll be here more in the summer than in the winter after the renovation work is complete. I still have cases, on and off, in London."

"Well, if I get any free time, you know I'll help you out."

Tasha appeared doubtful. "You? Free time? Do you *do* free time?"

"Ha ha." Yvonne accepted the hot tea with a broad smile.

"What you working on now, anyway?" Tasha grabbed two mis-matched wooden chairs, offering one to the DI.

Yvonne proceeded to fill Tasha in about Kate Nilsson's murder and the deaths which Kate had been looking into.

"Wow. Pretty complex. And I'm guessing it's uphill work, dealing with the army authorities.

"You could say that." The DI sighed. "I've got a couple of soldiers on the inside, giving me information." She pursed her lips. "Although sometimes, it is at godawful hours and in strange places." She thought of St Johns Priory, and spraying Dewi with mace.

"How far have you got?" Tasha's eyes narrowed. "Got any lead suspects?"

"Honestly?" Yvonne put her thumb between her teeth.

"No. Lie to me." Tasha giggled. "Of course, *honestly*."

"No."

"Oh."

"Exactly."

"Need any help?"

"Possibly. But I don't see how. You almost certainly wouldn't be allowed on the base, and two military police officers keep running off with possible pieces of evidence."

"I see."

"Dick and Harry, Dewi calls them."

Tasha smiled. "So what are you going to do? Have you any ideas where to look?"

"Well, I've been told to look at the officers and work up."

"I'm here, if there's anything I can do. Even if all you need is a brainstorming session."

"Thank you, Tasha. I appreciate it. Right now, I'm just enjoying being away from it all. Even if only for a few hours. Get my head straight."

She told Tasha about having to abandon Kim and her family and, most especially, her mum. She shed a few tears and felt better for it. Tasha listened with quiet understanding, until the DI had gotten it all out.

"Thank you, Tasha," The DI blew her nose.

"Any time." Tasha smiled.

.   .   .

IT WAS EARLY EVENING, by the time Yvonne headed home. She felt calm and more focused, if tired. It was strange going back to an empty house. She kicked off her shoes, made and ate beans on toast, then took the stairs to bed. This time, she slept.

~

RAIN AND SLEET had settled in again. Yvonne wore a mac over her jacket. Dai Clayton had thoughtfully brought the car round. She smiled at him. He was a traditional gentleman.

She ran out of the station and, holding her hood in place, threw open the car door to jump inside. "I doubt much work will be done up there." She pulled her hood back, mopping the rain off her face with a clean hanky.

"You'd be surprised," Clayton said, keeping his eyes on the road as he pulled out of Park Street junction. "They're on a tight schedule. I've seen parts of the site still working in worse than this. And I've been stuck in the traffic jams that have resulted."

"What does he do, this Sam Walters? I mean, what does he do on site?"

"Far as I know, ma'am, he's one of the foremen. Something to do with the initial area stripping."

"Oh, I see." She didn't, but wasn't about to admit it. "Does he know we're coming?"

"I spoke to him on the telephone this morning. He told me his break-time is around ten-thirty. We're ten minutes early but, by the time we find the pre-fab office, we'll be about right."

Dai parked the car at one end of the field.

Yvonne grabbed her bag. "I've come prepared." She

pulled out her notebook, running through the list of thoughts and questions she wanted to ask. She donned her wellingtons for the muddy tramp across the field.

THEY FOUND HIM EASILY, spotting his hard hat and high-vis, as they entered the field. He was carrying a clipboard and shouting to the other guys to take shelter. He made his way to the hut. He spotted them, and wandered over, his gait awkward. He struggled to meet their eyes.

"Sam?" Yvonne held out her hand.

He hesitated, and she thought he wasn't going to shake. He did, however, and held the hut door open for them to enter.

"Kettle's boiled," a young lad shouted to Sam, before leaving the hut.

Yvonne hoped the other men were either in their vehicles or another hut. The rain was now torrential.

"Yeah. I'm Sam." His voice was deep and husky. The DI thought it attractive. "How can I help you, officers?" He lined up three mugs. "Tea?"

Yvonne and her DC nodded.

"No sugar for me, please." Yvonne double-checked her notes. "Sam, I don't know if DS Clayton has already mentioned it, but we're here to discuss your time in the army."

"I know," he said, in hushed tones, keeping his back to them. His preparation of the tea had slowed.

"Specifically, we wanted to know about Helen Reynolds."

He stopped moving altogether, staring down at the brewing tea. "What would you like to know?" He sounded tired.

"What was she like?"

"Helen was lovely.' He poured milk into each mug and then turned to hand them theirs. "But I'm not sure she was cut out to be a soldier."

"What makes you say that?" Yvonne accepted her mug, warming her hands on it.

"She was headstrong and strong-willed. She constantly clashed with the NCOs, particularly Callaghan. She was attractive with it: fiery eyes and high cheek bones. She looked like a woman you wouldn't want to mess with. And yet, there was something about her that drove most of the regiment mad, wanting to get to know her better. If you get my drift."

"Did you want to know her better?" The DI studied his eyes.

"I did know her better." He looked down at his tea. "We dated for a short while, but she was too independent for a serious relationship. We quickly fizzled out."

"Were you disappointed?"

"I was and I wasn't" He took a big gulp of tea. "I hadn't expected it to work out, if I'm honest. Like I said, she was strong-minded and not the sort of girl you could pin down. I was happy to be her friend. She needed friends and was loyal to them."

"What about Callaghan? Why the clash with him?"

"He'd come on to her, after she first arrived at camp. She'd slapped his face. In my opinion, he never really forgave her for that. He and one or two other NCOs gave her a hard time."

"In what way?"

"Shouted at her on parade, gave her extra exercises and punishing physical workouts."

"How did she react?"

"She got on with it. She was never going to let them see her beaten. That's what she told me. She'd push herself every bit as hard as they pushed her, to prove to them that they couldn't break her." He turned to stare out the window, over the mud, flood water and silent machinery. "It was only afterwards that she would come and find me and...sob her heart out."

"Are you okay?" Yvonne put her mug on a little table, which wobbled, spilling some of the mug's contents.

"Me? Yeah. I'm fine." He sighed. "I was often the shoulder she cried on."

"What happened, the day she died?"

He closed his eyes for a couple of seconds. "I don't know. I mean, I don't know how it started. One of the lads came running to find me. It was an unusually hot day. Must have been thirty-five in the shade. He told me they were beasting Helen in the exercise hall, meaning they were punishing her for something. Making her do hard physical exercise. Well, the day was too bloody hot for that. What were they thinking? I ran over, to ask them - beg them - to stop. But I was too late. She'd already collapsed and a medic had been called. She was massively overheated. Her core temperature had rocketed."

"How did Callaghan react?"

"I don't know. I mean, I don't remember. I was too busy trying to help cool Helen down while we waited for the ambulance. I think he left the scene."

"You said officers, plural. Who was with him?"

"I don't... I'm not sure." He shook his head. "Could have been Staff-Sergeant Jones, but I couldn't swear. Like I said, I was too busy worrying about Helen."

"I'm sorry to ask." Yvonne leaned forward in her chair. "Did she die on the base?"

"She died in the hospital, but was probably already in multiple-organ failure by the time the ambulance got there."

"Was there an inquiry?"

"There was, and a report was published. They conceded it was a tragic accident. Like they couldn't have foreseen it. The officers got off with a warning and retraining. That was criminal in my book. They should have been done for murder."

"Well, perhaps manslaughter." Yvonne sighed. "Is that why you left the army?'

Sam's forehead furrowed at the question. "I'd lost my respect for them. I'd lost my faith in their ability to keep us safe. And, yes, it wasn't the same with Helen gone."

The DI nodded and got up to place a hand on his arm. "Thank you," she said in hushed tones. "That couldn't have been easy."

He shook his head. "I'm okay. I just hope you to bring her killers to justice."

THE RAIN STOPPED, as they left the hut and gingerly avoided the largest muddy puddles at the bottom of the steps.

"Do you think they knew she'd die?" DC Clayton was struggling to believe that could be the case.

"Who knows." Yvonne shook her head. "It could have been a tragic accident."

"But you don't think so?"

"I don't know, Dai. I don't know."

10

ANOTHER DEATH

Dewi came running to greet her, as she and Clayton pulled up in the car park.

"Ma'am." He was out of breath and panting hard. "They want to know if we want to go up to Chester."

"Why?" Yvonne screwed up her face.

"Cheshire police are at the priory. Stephen Whyte was found dead this morning."

"What?" The DI's hand flew to her chest, as she held her breath.

"His throat was slashed. A deep cut. He was almost decapitated, they're saying."

"Oh, no. No. No. No." She bent over, trying to get her breath and stop herself being sick. "I knew it. I knew it might be too big a risk. What was I thinking?"

Clayton and Dewi took an elbow each, and escorted Yvonne into the station.

She pulled her arms free. "We've got to get there. Are Dick and Harry still here?"

"Yes." Dewi nodded. "They're about to set off. We'll go in our car and meet them up there."

"Right." Yvonne was focused again, though deeply saddened by the news. "Before we go, could you ask the DCI to obtain clearance from Cheshire Police?"

"Will do, ma'am."

THE PRIORY WAS a hive of focussed activity when they arrived: police tape; cars with lights flashing; several ambulances and army personnel. People everywhere. The photographer had finished up and medics were about to go in to put Stephen into a body bag.

"Can we see him before you take him?" Yvonne asked one of the medics.

They paused in their tracks, shrugging and looking towards a superintendent from the Cheshire force. He was deep in conversation with Broderick Forster.

Yvonne flashed her ID at the medics, and they stepped to one side.

"He was terrified, Dewi." Yvonne turned to her DS. "Look at his eyes and mouth. Who had he seen?"

"There isn't much blood, considering." Dewi looked around. "He'd been hidden under those bushes. I reckon he was killed somewhere else, and then moved back here. The question is why?"

"This is my fault, Dewi. I asked to meet him here." Yvonne knelt next to the body. Her instincts were to touch his face. She stopped herself from doing that, but did put her hand on his. It was cold. The cold of the dead. A tear dropped from her lashes.

"Well, if I'm right," Dewi knelt down next to her, "it wouldn't have mattered where you met him. Looks like someone wanted him dead. Full stop."

"Yes, but to bring him here, Dewi. They had to have known I met him here."

"This may be their warning to you." Dewi stood again and held out his hand to help Yvonne up.

"They're warning me off." She felt angry. "It makes me all the more determined to hunt them down."

"Just look where they chose to leave him." Dewi pointed up at the priory tower. A wooden, human-shaped coffin was set, vertically, high in the tower. The inside of it was painted black. White letters inside read 'Dust to Dust'. Yvonne shuddered.

Dewi turned her to face him. "You may be in danger. Leaving his body here, and under that coffin, is their way of saying back off and leave things alone. Perhaps you should back off, for now. Let's think this through. Cheshire Police will investigate Stephen's murder. We can talk to them." Dewi put his hands on her shoulders.

She shrugged them off. "I'm not backing off. Several young soldiers have died at someone else's hands. I owe it to them and their families to find who is responsible. I can't walk away from this. Stephen Whyte put his life on the line and lost it trying to help us. We owe him."

"Okay. Okay. But let's regroup. Let's go through everything back at the station. Sort out what we've got and where to go next. If we're going to do this, we need planning and back-up, for if things go wrong. Llewellyn said we can liaise with Cheshire. He's allowing us to stay on the case. If we mess up, he could limit us to investigating only Kate's death."

Yvonne nodded. "You're right, Dewi. Just know that I'm not gong to give up."

. . .

SHE FELT NAUSEATED. Even now, her hands had a slight tremor. She joined Dewi with notebook and pens at the ready.

"Okay." Dewi sat with two coffees and a plate of digestives. "Suspects."

Yvonne grabbed a coffee and left the biscuits. "Sergeant Callaghan has to be high on the list. He had issues with several of the victims and had been coming on to Helen Reynolds and Kate Nilsson."

"And you said Stephen Whyte told you to look at him and Staff-Sergeant Jones first."

"That's right. And then work up. Broderick Forster. He's got to be on the list, though I find it hard to believe that he, himself, would have committed any of the murders."

"Right. But he could have ordered them."

"Maybe, but why? What did all the victims have in common? What made *them* targets."

"Something they'd seen? Maybe something out in the field: Iraq or Afghanistan. Maybe another war theatre."

"I like your thinking. So, something like prisoner torture?"

"Or the illegal killing of prisoners, maybe."

Yvonne pulled a face.

"It's just a thought."

"If that's what happened, whoever was in charge would want it covered up. Could be career-ending."

"To be honest," Dewi scratched his head, "we've got a whole battalion of potential suspects, and the leadership goes right up to the MOD, and even the queen.

Yvonne raised an eyebrow. "I think we can rule out Her Majesty."

"Yeah, but she is the commander-in-chief of the forces, isn't she?" He gave her a big wink.

"Very funny." Yvonne tapped him on the arm with her pad. "Seriously, though. We've got to keep digging around the victims' lives and backgrounds. Something links them. Until we find out what that is, we're unlikely to crack this case. Our way in is Kate. We've got to find out what she knew."

"Agreed. I think we should speak to Lars and Hayley Nilsson again. You said you felt they were hiding something. Just maybe, Kate fed back more to them than they are letting on."

"Let's do it." Yvonne downed the rest of her drink, as the door swung open and Chris Llewellyn entered in a hurry.

"Come with me, guys, we've got a copy of the CCTV footage from Cheshire. The one you requested I ask for."

"You got it?" Yvonne's eyes shone. This was very good news.

"I did. I can also tell you that early results suggest Corporal Whyte was killed two nights before he was found. Come on."

Yvonne and Dewi exchanged glances. Two nights before put his death the night Yvonne met him at the Priory.

LLEWELLYN HELD the door open for them to go first. "Cheshire are saying there's a possible suspect on the CCTV. They're working on cleaning it up to get a good visual."

The rest of the team were already assembled and eagerly awaiting the footage from the DCI.

"Just got to get into my emails." Llewellyn sat at the screen, to begin downloading the files. "Here we go."

There was footage following Stephen en route to the Priory, walking through Chester and along part of the wall.

He was continually looking over his shoulder and walking quickly.

"Looks scared, doesn't he? Like he knew he was being followed. He knew someone was after him." DC Clayton put his hands deep in his pockets, eyes narrowed.

Yvonne shifted from foot to foot. She ran a hand through her hair several times, sweat developing on her upper lip.

The footage at the priory was black and white and grainy. It caught Stephen as he entered the grounds, before he appeared to melt into the shadows.

The next bit of footage was clearly from another camera. It showed the approach to the priory from the street. A figure came into view and the DI held her breath. Heart racing, she could feel the heat in her cheeks, as they filled with blood. A cold tingle travelled down her spine.

"It's a female, isn't it? Definitely a woman." Callum Jones leaned in towards the screen.

"You're right." Llewellyn frowned, pausing the file. "Let me just check the email. Er...suspect comes into frame at nineteen hundred hours. Yes, this has to be the suspect. Damn it being so grainy. But a woman? Are we seriously saying that this woman inflicted those injuries on Corporal Whyte?" Llewellyn rubbed his forehead.

"We'll have to find out who she is." Clayton shrugged. "Well, Cheshire will. Look, she's meeting with Whyte in the priory grounds."

Yvonne watched as she and Corporal Whyte disappeared back into the shadows, remembering that he had pulled her into them. He had known where the CCTV cameras were.

The footage cut out shortly after.

"Is that it?" Clayton asked in frustration.

"I'm afraid so." Llewellyn reread the email. "They said

there was a problem with the camera after that. There's no more footage from that night."

"You have to be kidding." Dai Clayton slapped his hands on his thighs. "Of all the rotten luck. Not that the footage was great, but still."

"We've got to find out who that woman was." DCI Llewellyn sat back in his chair.

Dewi looked at Yvonne, who cleared her throat.

"Sir," she began tentatively, clearing her throat again. "The woman in the footage is me."

"What?" It took a second or two for him to fully register, then: "My office. Now."

The DI turned on her heel. She could feel a cold sweat on her skin. Behind her back, soft murmurs broke out amongst the team.

"You've got some explaining to do, Yvonne." LLewellyn's eyes bored into her. The colour in his cheeks heightened as he stood, both hands on hips.

She swallowed hard. Words wouldn't come.

"What were you doing in Chester at that time, talking to a soldier in some dark churchyard? A soldier who is subsequently murdered. Maybe because he talked to you. How did that happen? How was that not on my radar? Why wasn't I aware of this?"

She felt like a naughty schoolchild, not sure of which question to answer first. "I'm sorry," was all she managed.

"Is that it? I'm sorry? You'd better start talking to me, Yvonne. I've got to get on that phone and tell Cheshire that their number one suspect-stroke-witness in a case just happens to be one of my officers and I didn't even know you were there. Did you go alone?"

"No, sir." She shifted her weight between her feet. "Dewi was with me. Well, he was in the car, waiting."

"So, you *and* Dewi were there. Well, I suppose that's something." He gave a heavy sigh. "I mean, you could have been at risk. Why were you meeting Corporal Whyte in the priory?"

"He requested that location. I wanted to talk to him and he felt it was too risky at the base. He chose the time and the place."

"And you just went along with it. No thought to speak to me or to request proper backup. What if he'd attacked you? What if his killer had killed you too?"

"I think his death may have been a warning to me." Hot tears coursed down her cheeks.

"Oh, for heaven's sake." He ran his hands through his hair. "Are you saying you think he was killed because he talked to you?"

"I think it's possible. More than likely."

"Here..." He handed her a clean hanky. "What did you want from him? Did he have information about Kate Nilsson?"

She dried her eyes and blew her nose. "No. Not directly."

"Then what did you hope to gain?"

"He had been friends with two of the young soldiers who died in suspicious circumstances. Deaths which Kate had been investigating before she was killed."

"You should have spoken to me, Yvonne. You could have told me what you were planning."

"You'd have stopped me."

He ignored the last. "And what about Thornton and Simmonds? Where were they?"

"They didn't know."

"Well, they're just going to be cock-a-hoop about that."

He fell silent, as though all the energy had been drained from him. Or perhaps he'd lost his thread. After what seemed like an age, he added, "That'll be all. I'm going to have a think about whether you need a vacation or a case reassignment."

"But-"

"I'll come and find you, later."

There was so much she wanted to say. The words just would not come. She felt as though she deserved everything she got. A young man was dead, probably because he talked to her. She needed to get her head straight. She went to find Dewi.

As she passed colleagues, there was a hushed silence. She sensed commiseration from some and judgement from others. Perhaps she did need a break. There was still time to see her family.

11

SECOND WIND

S he sat at her desk, head in hands. Most of her colleagues had gone home. Dewi had done his best to console her, but she was cloaked in despondency, and the feeling that she had let everybody down. Most of all the victims.

DCI Llewellyn entered and shut the door behind him.

Yvonne jumped, looking at him through half-lidded eyes.

"I've spoken with Cheshire." He perched on the edge of her desk, looking down at her, almost like he were her parent. "They're not amused that their suspect turned out to be one of us. Luckily, they're not dwelling on it. They're more concerned that the CCTV appears to have been turned off. There was a power outage. Someone tampered with a service box. The footage cuts out directly after your conversation with Stephen." He rubbed his chin. "They want to meet with you. Find out what you remember and whether you saw anyone else."

"Are you taking me off the case?"

"I should."

Yvonne looked down at her hands.

"But, no. I'm not taking you off the case. But *please* work with Thornton and Simmonds and keep them, and me, informed. Understood?"

"Understood. Thank you." She looked up at him.

His eyes were soft. "I know you think they won't be impartial, but they are supposed to be independent investigators and we *have* to trust that they are."

"I know."

"Go home, Yvonne. Get some rest. Don't blame yourself for Corporal Whyte's death. Just find his killer and do it safely."

She nodded and rose, to head out. She was glad of the chance to leave. She didn't want to cry again.

SHE HAD TO REFOCUS. Get her head and the investigation back on track. She felt determined as she walked down the corridor. She'd go back to the beginning. It irked her that she could not investigate Stephen Whyte's death directly, but Kate Nilsson's was a different matter. The key to whatever evil lay behind these murders lay with Kate. She felt she owed it to Private Nilsson, to know what she knew. To walk in her footsteps.

She phoned Kim as soon as she arrived home. She spoke to them all: her sister, her mum and the children. She felt better for it. She listened as they told her about their Christmas celebrations and New Year's resolutions. It was good to talk to them. Ground herself. She made another promise to be back with them soon, and this time, she was going to keep it.

❧

THE MANILLA FOLDER WAS BACK. So were Dick and Harry. Dewi ran up two flights of stairs to find the DI, waving the yellow folder in his hand.

Her eyes lit up and she ran to meet him. Dewi put it on the table and the two of them stared at it, like a Christmas present they were afraid to open, in case the contents were a disappointment.

"Let's do it." Yvonne grabbed the folder and pulled out the papers.

"Resumés?" She handed Dewi the top one. "These are copies of the personnel files of Kevin McEwan, Helen Reynolds and Tom Rendon." The DI began flicking through. "Looks like we have their whole career, from induction through to their deaths."

Dewi pursed his lips. "How on earth had Kate Nilsson got her hands on these?"

"Quite. More importantly, why did she need them?" Yvonne continued flicking through Kevin's file, just as Dick and Harry entered the room.

"See? Told you we'd get it back to you ASAP." Simmonds looked pleased with himself. "It had to have clearance. Those files are MOD property and confidential."

"Very little has been redacted." The DI's eyes narrowed.

Thornton crossed over to stand behind Yvonne. "Well, they wouldn't hide anything they didn't need to." He smiled. "I knew you'd be pleased about that."

Yvonne couldn't help her feelings. The lack of redaction increased her suspicion. "Can we hang onto these for a while?" She closed the pages she was reading. She didn't want to study them in front of the RMP officers. No matter what the DCI said.

"You can have them for a couple of weeks. After that, the

ministry will want them destroyed, which they will do themselves."

"Destroyed?" Dewi looked wide-eyed at them.

"These have been printed from the digital files. It's not clear who printed them, but they are surplus to requirements and shouldn't exist." He gave Dewi a 'hello' sort of a look.

Dewi looked away. Yvonne could see that his clenched knuckles were white.

"We don't keep paper copies of personnel files much these days." Thornton appeared to want to make up for his colleague's lack of sensitivity. "All records are digital. Private Nilsson somehow obtained printouts. That is being investigated, as we speak. In the meantime, because they had been in Kate's possession, they have been returned to you. But I must ask that you keep access to these files limited."

Yvonne nodded, grateful and surprised that she had received them back, at all.

THEY WERE, once more, on their way to Chester. Yvonne dreaded having to face Cheshire police. She knew she would feel foolish, throughout. It would also delay her speaking again with Sergeants Callaghan and Jones, and meeting the regimental-sergeant, Major Robert Wyn-Thomas, the most senior-ranked NCO.

It felt strange, and plain wrong, to be on the other side of the interview table. The two detectives from Cheshire gave the date and names for the tape. Yvonne felt sick.

They made her a cup of tea and she sipped it rapidly.

"So, Detective Inspector Giles, tell us how you came to know Corporal Stephen Whyte."

Yvonne sighed. "Am I seriously on your suspect list?"

"You're not very high up the list, if that's any consolation." The older detective eyed her and she sensed an empathy.

"But you were the last known person to see him alive." The younger detective's demeanour was firmer, perhaps suspecting she may be corrupt.

"Corporal Whyte asked to meet me there. As you know, I was investigating the death of one of his army colleagues, Kate Nilsson. She was killed while out for a run, near her family home."

"You thought he had information about the murder? Why not pull him in for questioning? Why not refer him to us?"

"Kate was looking into suspicious deaths at the barracks." Yvonne's eyes lingered on the rolled-up sleeves of the younger detective. "Something is scaring soldiers at that barracks. Corporal Whyte wanted to meet me off base. He chose the time and the venue. I don't know why he chose the priory."

"But you talked to him."

"I did."

"What did he say to you?"

Yvonne paused. Could she trust them? "He said he doubted the findings of the inquests into previous deaths at the base."

"Our force was fully involved in investigations. The findings by both ourselves, and the army, were thorough and comprehensive. No foul-play was detected. You're wasting your time if you think you'll find any different."

"I didn't say that was what I was trying to do."

"So, what were you doing questioning him?"

"Kate Nilsson's death was not suicide."

"We could have provided back-up. We could have helped protect you and Corporal Whyte."

Yvonne doubted that. She doubted it very much. Since Corporal Whyte was killed away from the priory, and brought back there. She was sure it was done to ward her off. "So, am I really a suspect? Or are you getting revenge because I didn't consult with you?"

"Did you see anyone else? Anyone at all, in the area?"

She pursed her lips. "No. No-one. I was feeling on edge and would have been aware. I heard people in the far distance. I heard a dog barking. I saw no-one. That is, until my DS arrived and I maced him in the face."

The younger detective stifled a laugh.

"Why did you do that?"

"I was anxious."

"So, you knew the situation could be a dangerous one."

"I suffer with anxiety. I have occasional panic attacks. Dark places always have me on edge."

"So what happened after you maced your DS in the face?"

"I took him to the hospital."

"So, there'll be witnesses to that."

"Quite a few. I think we amused the hospital staff that evening."

More smirks from the younger detective. "You *were* feeling nervous, weren't you?"

"Well, meeting him like that - in the dark. I bet you'd have been on edge, too."

"Without back-up, I would."

The older detective interjected. "Look, did you see anyone near the cameras? Anyone climbing up anywhere, anything like that?"

"No."

"Would you have seen anyone if they were there?"

"Yes. No. Don't know." She shook her head, self-doubt creeping back. Perhaps she had missed something.

The older detective pushed his chair back. "You're free to go."

"That's it? Am I still a suspect?"

"No. You never were. Not really."

"Then why all this?"

"You took risks with yours and the victim's safety."

"I feel terrible about Stephen's death. I regret not having had the area staked out." She sighed heavily. "Perhaps we should have given him a lift back to the base."

They nodded, and the younger detective smiled at her. "Remind me never to go on an op with you, if you have mace in your pocket."

Was that supposed to make her feel better? She smiled weakly, but inside she was furious. Someone was pulling the strings. They had manipulated her and taken the life of another victim. She'd been set up and humiliated, and the puppet-master was still at large.

As she walked down the corridor, away from the two detectives, that anger morphed into steely determination. Her footfall became stronger and more regular. As she left the building, and the winter sun lit her face, she knew exactly what she would do. She'd bring in Tashsa. She'd somehow get Tasha into Dale.

12

TASHA COMES ON BOARD

Yvonne's breath curled and twisted in the frosted air, as she and Dewi walked the path towards the Nilsson's home in Llydiart. Frost clothed the hedgerows and fields in ephemeral white. It had the beauty of snow, without the complications.

Her rap on the front door was loud and firm. Lars had some explaining to do.

Lars opened the door, surprised at finding the two detectives at his door again. They hadn't phoned. His expression quickly turned to expectation.

"Anything?" he asked, eyebrows raised.

Yvonne shook her head. "Not yet."

The corners of Lars' mouth turned down.

"We've come to ask you a few more questions, Lars." Her eyes searched his face.

"Questions about what? My wife is asleep upstairs, we'll have to keep our voices down." He took them through to the kitchen and pulled up chairs next to the Aga.

Yvonne pulled out her notebook. "Lars, you said Kate had been looking into suicides at the base."

"Yes…"

"Did *you* ask her to do that?"

He looked down at his feet.

The DI glanced at Dewi, who had continued standing. Hands in pockets. Legs apart, as though ready for a sparring session.

She continued, "I think you encouraged your daughter to delve deeper into what happened, and we," Yvonne glanced at her DS, as he nodded affirmation, "suspect she was feeding information back to you."

His eyes narrowed.

"We're not judging you. We just want to know what you know. We want you to tell us what it was she found out."

"Would you believe me if I told you that she closed up? Since the early weeks of her investigations, she said little. It was like she was trying to protect us. Actually, I know she was trying to protect us. She told me. She said she thought she was on to something big and didn't want to put us in danger."

Yvonne rubbed her chin.

"No, really. She gave me the impression that powerful people were involved. People who could make problems go away."

"Did she give you anything to go on? Anything at all?"

Lars sighed and looked about, as though he felt eyes on him. "There's a box," he said, finally, "upstairs in Kate's room. In the bottom of her wardrobe. She told me to keep it safe."

"May we see it?"

"Come on, I'll show you. But please be quiet. As I explained, my wife is sleeping."

Yvonne and Dewi slipped off their shoes and followed Lars upstairs.

The box was a small one that had originally contained envelopes. Lars removed the lid. Inside, were several photographs of Kate on her own and with others. All were taken in the same street. The street could have been anywhere. In the background were shops, parked cars, and a partial sign above what appeared to be a coffee shop. The only letter legible on the partial sign was a large S. The way the photographer had taken the photo, was such that the rest of the name was missing. Both Dewi and Yvonne took turns studying the photographs, to see if they could recognise the place. They couldn't. In one, Kate was flanked by Steven Whyte and Wayne Hedges. Arms around each other's shoulders, they looked like they were having fun. Same street, but a night-time shot.

"Do you know where these were taken?" Yvonne asked Lars.

"I'm sorry, I don't." Lars scratched his head. "It's nowhere I'm familiar with."

"May we keep them a while?" Yvonne's gaze was softer, now. This was a big thing for Lars: handing over something which his dead daughter had asked him to keep safe. Perhaps she had misjudged him.

"Yes. Yes, of course." Lars handed her the box. "Could I please have them back when you've finished?"

Yvonne nodded. "I'll make sure we look after them." She gave him a warm smile and placed a reassuring hand on his elbow.

He led them back downstairs and showed them out.

"How on earth do we find out where those were taken?" Dewi beeped his key-fob at the car.

"I don't know, Dewi, but we can start by asking the team to scan the images. See what they come up with. Failing that, I could approach Wayne Hedges." She frowned. "Though, after what happened to Stephen-"

"We'll start with the team." Dewi's nod was emphatic. "Let's see what they come up with."

~

THE DRIVE to Aberdovey went by in a haze. Yvonne's head was full of images and snippets of conversations. She pulled into Tasha'a yard and was greeted by the psychologist, who handed her a glass of white. She gratefully accepted it. "It's okay to stay the night, then?"

"Of course." Tasha grinned. "The spare room is ready. It has an excellent view of the sea, and dinner is cooking."

Yvonne began to relax. Tiredness washed over her. The kind which washes over someone when they've had to be strong under fire, and they see a friendly face.

A tear escaped and ran down her face.

"Hey. Hey, what's wrong? Come here."

Tasha grabbed hold of her friend and gave her a long hug. The chill of the evening air stung their faces and Tasha guided the DI inside.

"I'm fine, It's just so good to take a few hours out. It's been a tough few days."

"Want to talk about it?"

"Maybe, eventually. But not now."

Tasha smiled. "No worries. You know I'm here, if you want to."

The psychologist lit candles around the room and dimmed the lights. "Come on." She took a sip from her glass. "Let's watch the moon on the water, while we wait for the food to finish cooking."

They sat on lounge cushions, on the floor in front of the massive sliding doors. Tasha got up to put some light jazz on. They sipped their wine, while the smells from the kitchen grew ever-more enticing.

Neither spoke. Maybe Tasha sensed that was what Yvonne needed, and a relaxed silence was easy with the DI.

The moon, bold and strong, danced on the water. Forming, breaking, and reforming. Yvonne thought of the moonrakers - an ancient people, who believed they could catch the moon from the water's surface with their nets. They could only break it into a myriad shards, however, each time their nets broke the surface. The moon had parallels with the answers to her case.

"I messed up. A young man died." As she said the words, she continued to stare out of the window, knees against her chest, chin pressed against the rim of her glass.

Tasha turned to look at her and, realising her friend was still trying to get her head around something, turned back to watch the sea. Her eyes followed the silhouettes of the boulders and rocks, on down to the sand and sea. "Do you want to talk about it?"

"Yes. But I'm not sure where to start."

"You're chasing another killer."

"Killer or killers. Could be one, could be a shadowy web."

"I see."

"If I have to narrow it down, then I'm after the person who pulled the trigger and murdered a female soldier in her mum and dad's back yard, in cold blood." The DI continued until she had poured it all out. As she finished, the tension eased away.

"Why do you blame yourself for Corporal Whyte's

death?" Tasha asked the question in hushed tones, fearful her friend might clam up again.

"I thought his talking to me might put him in danger. That's why I let him choose the place and time. I thought he had an idea who was doing the killing."

"He would have known he was putting himself in danger. He wouldn't have met you if he thought it wouldn't be worth the risk. He wanted justice for his friends. He wanted that, even if it put his life in danger. He had faith in you. It's your job now to make sure that he, and they, get that justice, and I know you can do it. Stop wallowing now, please, and get down to doing what you do best. Bring the guilty in." Tasha reached out to put a hand on her friend's shoulder. "Is there anything I can do to help?"

"Actually, I was going to ask you if you'd like to be involved. I would dearly love for you to come and talk to some of those characters on that base. Get your take on them."

"Okay. Let's do it."

"It's not going to be that easy. I doubt you'd get clearance as an unofficial psychologist. I don't think you'd get past army security or RMP officers, Dick and Harry."

"Dick and Harry?" Tasha laughed. "Is that their real names?"

"Yeah." Yvonne grinned. "They're from the Military Police Special Investigations Unit."

"Oh, I see."

"Anything I do on the base has to be with them or fully endorsed by them. And, since what happened with Corporal Whyte, I'm on a very tight leash."

"So how do we go about it? Covert video?"

Yvonne grimaced.

"How about I masquerade as one of your team. DC Tasha Phillips has a certain ring to it." Tasha grinned.

Yvonne sat bolt-upright. "You know, that might just work. We could let Dewi in on it. Dick and Harry haven't met my whole team. They won't know any different. Hopefully, they would leave us to it. The guards at the entrance know myself and Dewi, they wave us through. We'll show a badge. That should be enough."

"I could blag that I'd left my badge at the station."

"Okay, let me sleep on it. First, though, I think I need to sample that delicious-smelling food you've got going on in there. If you make me wait any longer, I'll pass out."

After dinner, they walked along the beach for an hour or so, wrapped up like eskimos. It cleared both their minds, and Yvonne had to admit to feeling a million times better. When they got back, the DI's mobile was bleating loudly inside her bag.

Expecting it to be Dewi, she was surprised that the caller was Private Wayne Hedges. "Wayne?"

He sounded breathless. "They got to Stephen, didn't they?"

"They? Who's they?"

"If they're worried about what he said to you, they'll be after you, too." He hung up, leaving a shocked Yvonne staring at her mobile.

"Everything all right?" Tasha took the mobile out of her hand.

"That was Private Wayne Hedges. I think he was warning me that I'm in danger."

"Is he right?" Tasha frowned. "That's not good."

"Probably no more than I deserve." The DI clenched her hands. "Well, bring it on. I'm a police officer. I have a whole team behind me. I've faced danger before, it's nothing new. I'm going to find the murderer of these young soldiers, even if it kills me. I'm not going to be put off."

Tasha gave her friend a hug. "Right, I'm going to that base with you."

13

FAKE DETECTIVE

S taff-Sergeant Jones gave Yvonne a stern look, as she and Tasha entered Forster's office. He ushered them in faster than he would normally and there was a stiffness about him, like there was somewhere else he needed to be.

Broderick Forster rose from his desk and came over to shake their hands. He was in military fatigues.

"Major-General Forster, I've brought another member of my team today. This is Tasha Phillips."

"Tasha."

The psychologist's smile was broad and relaxed.

"Tasha and I have worked several successful cases together. She's an excellent member of my team."

"Pleased to meet you." Forster held onto her hand. He gave her a warm smile. "So," his attention returned to Yvonne. "How are you getting on with with SIB?"

Yvonne thought about her answer. There was so much she wanted to say. Instead, she settled for, "Fine. I'm quite surprised they're not already here, actually. They were supposed to be meeting us."

Forster called Staff-Sergeant Jones. "Can you check if the RMPs have arrived on base?"

"Sir." Staff-Sergeant Jones saluted and left.

The DI felt a sense of relief.

"So, how can I help you today, Inspector Giles?" Forster flicked his gaze between Yvonne and Tasha.

"With your permission, we'd like to speak with Staff-Sergeant Jones and Sergeant Callaghan. We'd also like to see Kate's room again, if possible. Also..." She took out her notebook. "Are there any other officers who would have had direct contact with Kate Nilsson? Any who might give further insight? I have the name Robert Wyn-Thomas in my book."

Forster rubbed his chin, clicking his tongue. "Hmm. Rob Wyn-Thomas is the RSM. That is, the Regimental Sergeant-Major. He's the most senior of my NCOs. He has responsibility for the whole battalion. He's also one of my most senior advisors."

"Would he be available to speak to us?"

"I'll have one of my men find out where he is." With that, Forster picked up his phone and barked instruction down it.

Yvonne gave Tasha a wink. So far, so good.

STAFF-SERGEANT JONES ACCOMPANIED them to Kate's room. He didn't speak, as he led them down Kate's barrack block corridor. Once he got to Kate's door, however, he turned to face them. "Where's Thornton?"

The question took the DI by surprise. She searched his clean-shaven face. His expression impassive, he paused with the keys in the lock.

"Didn't you manage to find them?" Yvonne asked, wide-eyed.

"No, I didn't." It was an accusation. "They haven't been through the gate. Shouldn't you wait until they get here?"

"Oh, I'm sure they'll be here any minute. We've been through the room with them, previously. There will be nothing they haven't already seen. We just want to take another look, for the sake of completion, and to remind ourselves about the victim."

He still hadn't turned the key in the lock and, for a horrible moment, Yvonne thought he wasn't going to let them in. However, he did turn the key, and took a step back.

"Thank you." The DI stepped into the room, quickly followed by Tasha. "We'll be about twenty minutes."

He stood at the door and Yvonne was afraid he was going to stay there. She heard laughter and voices from down the corridor. Staff-Sergeant Jones turned on his heel and she closed the door and leaned on it.

"Phew." Tasha blew out a large breath, puffing her cheeks. "Thought he was never going to leave."

Yvonne took a a bunch of photographs from her bag. "Tasha, these are prints of photographs found on Kate's mobile phone. It seems she repeatedly took photographs of her room over several months." She scattered them on the surface of Kate's bed.

"Are they all the same?" Tasha had begun to peruse them.

"Yes, they are, as far as I can tell. They're pictures of this room, and all from two, slightly different, perspectives."

"Okay…" Tasha divided them into two groups. "Why so many, and why the two perspectives?"

Yvonne sat on the edge of the bed. "Beats me. Except, I think she may have been recording the scene so she'd know if anything had been disturbed."

"Was she a keen photographer?" Tasha pursed her lips, tapping one of the photographs against them.

"I don't know." Yvonne frowned. "Why do you ask?"

"Rule of thirds. You make the object of interest, in a photo or painting, two-thirds of the way in and two-thirds of the way up. It's where the eyes like to fall."

"What are you saying?"

"Well, even though these two groups are of slightly altered perspective, they have the same wall picture at the sweet spot."

"Oh, I see." Yvonne looked at the photographs, and then the actual picture on the wall, walking over to take a closer look.

It was a photograph of Kate with Wayne Hedges and Stephen Whyte. They had their arms around each other's shoulders and were smiling into the camera. It looked like it was taken at some sort of ball night. The guys wore tuxedos and Kate, a shimmering dress. It could have been several years ago, they looked like teenagers. The caption read 'James Bond Casino Night, 2010."

The DI read the caption aloud.

"Did something happen that night?" Tasha asked, looking around the rest of Kate's room.

"I don't know." Yvonne shook her head. "The only person still alive in that photo is Wayne Hedges."

"Maybe we should talk to him." Tasha walked back to the photos on the bed.

"Let me think about it. I do need to talk to him, but don't want to put him at risk." She sighed, gathering the photographs. "I still think she was monitoring her room."

As they checked through the rest of the room, Yvonne told Tasha about the Manilla folder, with the personnel files, and its connection to the soldiers who died on the base.

"So, why had she obtained copies of the personal files?" Tasha scratched her head. "What was she looking for?"

"I don't know, but there was obviously something in their histories which interested her. We examined the files. There was nothing obvious, aside from the fact they all joined the army at the same time. All three of them. Scotty McEwan, Helen Reynolds and Tom Rendon. They were a similar age. They'd been to pretty much the same war theatres. It's no surprise that they formed a strong friendship."

Tasha nodded. "It would have been a tight bond. Joining up together, going through the trials of basic training and adjusting to army life and fighting together. Those sorts of bonds last a lifetime."

"Especially when those lifetimes are cut short. Yvonne gazed through Kate's window with hollow eyes.

"Staff-Sergeant Jones will be back at any moment." Tasha glanced at her watch.

Yvonne nodded. "I expect this room will be cleared soon. Kate's things will be returned to her family."

As though on cue, there was a rap on the door and Staff-Sergeant Jones walked in. He had Simmonds with him. Yvonne paled.

Simmonds walked up to her and shook her hand. "Everything all right, here?" Staff-Sergeant Jones explained you were here. Came to see if you needed any help." He looked at Tasha, as though waiting for an introduction. None came.

"We're just finishing in here, actually," Yvonne's tone was clipped. "We were about to speak with Staff-Sergeant Jones. Also, Sergeant Callaghan and the RSM, Robert Wyn-Jones."

Sergeant Jones looked surprised. "What about?" he asked, rubbing his forearm.

"Oh, a few things. For example, weapons smuggling, when soldiers are returning from assignments abroad. Also, the whereabouts of officers and men, when Stephen Whyte was killed."

"Corporal Whyte?" Simmonds interjected. "That's not your case. Not your jurisdiction." He smiled, but it felt like a threat.

"We're working with Cheshire Police." It wasn't a lie. "There's more than a possibility that Stephen and Kate's deaths are linked. We are working to that premise."

Simmonds looked at Tasha and his eyes narrowed.

Tasha appeared remarkably calm. "A killer is taking down members of this regiment." Tasha eyed him with clear, piercing eyes. "We don't know where he, or she, will strike next. It's in everybody's interest to cooperate with this investigation." She turned her attention to Jones. "Except for the killer's, of course."

Yvonne was impressed with Tasha's performance. Hell, she'd make a good DC.

"I FELT LIKE A NAUGHTY SCHOOLGIRL." Tasha leaned back against the toilet cubicle. "I feel like any moment now they'll realise I'm an imposter."

"You handled that really well. And, so far, we've managed to avoid having to give a job description for you. So we haven't really lied to anyone. But, I do wonder what the hell I'm doing. I feel like I'm losing my grip. I don't think it has ever been so difficult to investigate a case. It's like I'm doing it with my ankles tied and my hands behind my back. And anyone I interview could become a victim."

"You need to speak with Wayne Hedges, though I understand your reluctance." Tasha headed for the door back to the corridor. "Come on. Let's start with those NCOs. You ask the questions and I'll observe. I'll tell you what I think, later. Make sure you ask them, specifically, what they think happened to Kate and Stephen."

Sergeant Callaghan's pace stick was tucked under his arm, having just put his platoon through their paces. He walked over as soon as he saw them. Simmonds hovered behind, sipping coffee from a paper cup.

"Inspector Giles." Callaghan's stiff back gave him an air of self-importance, but he smiled openly at them.

"Sergeant Callaghan, is it all right to talk to you now?" Yvonne shot a glance behind her, at Simmonds. His eyes watched her over his paper cup.

"Certainly. How can I help you?" Callaghan drew alongside.

"When you've been on tour, for example Bosnia, Iraq or Afghanistan, have you been aware of any of your troops smuggling back weaponry to the UK?"

Callaghan frowned. "It has happened. It's rare, though. Are you asking this because of the weapon used to kill Private Nilsson?"

"Yes. What do you know about that weapon?"

"I know you've identified it as a Bosnian pistol."

"And how would you know that?"

"Ole Forster, himself. He said that's what you told him."

"Is it possible someone on this base has been in possession of such a weapon since your tours of Bosnia?"

He nodded. "It's possible, though I'm not saying it's likely."

"Sergeant Callaghan, last time I spoke to you, you told me about an argument Kate had with Private Billy Rawlins, a few days before her death. Have you any idea what that row was about?"

"Afraid not, Inspector. When I got there, they had ceased arguing and were talking quietly. The rumour was that Rawlins had a crush on her and she was putting him off."

"Might we speak with Private Rawlins?"

He tapped the brass tip of his pace stick a couple of times on the floor. "I'm sure the argument had nothing to do with Kate's death."

"Sure? What makes you so sure?" Yvonne cocked her head to one side.

"Okay." He sighed. "What I meant was, I *doubt* the argument had anything to do with Private Nilsson's death."

"So, may we speak with him?"

"Very well. I'll have him meet you in one of the offices in one hour."

The DI nodded her appreciation. "Thank you, Sergeant Callaghan." She exchanged glances with Tasha, then added, "Sergeant Callaghan, can I ask where you were the night Stephen Whyte was murdered?"

He turned to face her directly, breathing out very slowly, before asking, "Am I a suspect?"

"One of many," Yvonne said, truthfully.

He shook his head. "What did Corporal Whyte say to you?" There was a steeliness to his delivery.

"He said I should start by looking at the officers." Her own delivery was calm and direct.

Callaghan frowned. "Did he?" he asked, but it was rhetorical, as he wandered away.

IT WAS the first time that Yvonne had met the Regimental Sergeant-Major. Robert Wyn-Thomas was not at all how she expected. She had imagined him with a full and twirling moustache, greying sandy hair, and tall. In fact, he was of average height, clean-shaven and dark-haired, with only a hint of grey developing at his temples.

He was buried in paperwork, and appeared to be pouring over battle plans.

"Planning exercises," he explained, when he saw them craning their necks to see.

"Should we come back at a better time?" Yvonne could feel Simmonds breath on the back of her neck, as she stood next to Tasha, just inside the office doorway.

"No. No, it's fine. I was about to take a break, anyway."

"How long have you been in the army?" Yvonne asked. She'd read that an RSM was at the pinnacle of his army career and would be nearing army retirement age.

"Twenty-seven years." He stifled a yawn. "I'll be retiring next year."

"You must have seen a lot." Yvonne felt awkward at probably the understatement of the year.

"Been to every war theatre the UK has been involved in, since 1987. That includes Northern Ireland."

"Wow." She was genuinely impressed. "So, that would include Bosnia?"

"Bosnia, Iraq, Afghanistan, Africa and Europe - in peacetime."

"Can I ask if you were aware of weaponry being smuggled back from any of these places. Any of your men caught doing it?"

"It went on, if that's what you mean. We stamp on it,

though. Anyone involved is punished and the weapons confiscated, when we find out. The soldiers face jail-time. Mostly, it's been fairly innocent. American troops gave our boys some stuff, from boots and other bits of kit, to the occasional hand gun. Why do you ask?"

"Kate Nilsson was killed with a 1990's-issue Bosnian pistol."

Simmonds perched on a chair, against the wall. He was busily making his own notes. Yvonne found that strangely annoying.

The RSM rubbed his face. "I heard rumours that weapons had been taken, it was a bit of a free-for-all, at times. But I never found any. If some *were* taken, by any of our men, they were well-hidden."

"How well did you know Private Nilsson?"

"Kate? I knew her as well as I know any of the soldiers in my regiment. But I didn't know her beyond that."

"Did you know Scotty McEwan, Tom Rendon and Helen Reynolds?"

He looked at her as though she had slapped him. "Yes."

Simmonds made a loud throat-clearing noise, as he looked up from his notes.

"Why do you ask that?" The RSM frowned.

"We found copies of their personnel files amongst Kate's belongings." Yvonne kept her tone matter-of-fact.

"If I hadn't before, I came to know them *very* well after their deaths."

"So, you didn't know them that well before their deaths?"

"I knew them, of course. But only as well as I know every other young soldier in my command. I was Scotty's platoon sergeant, so I knew him better than the others. What has all that to do with Kate's death?"

"Maybe nothing, but I believe she was carrying out an unofficial investigation into their deaths before she was killed."

"You think that's why she died." It was a statement, not a question.

"I think that it's at least possible the two are connected, yes."

"Kate was a very popular soldier." He folded his arms. "Especially with the men."

"You mean romantically?"

"I'd say it's just as likely she was killed by a jealous lover or wannabe lover. And that could have been a civilian just as well as a fellow soldier."

"But that brings us back to the weapon that was used. The 1990's Kosovan pistol. Ballistics have confirmed the ammunition. Also 1990's Kosovan."

"You can get anything on the black market-"

"Hmm." Yvonne pursed her lips. "I wasn't aware of Kate having a boyfriend. Did you have anyone specific in mind?"

"No, but Callaghan told me he'd seen her having a spat with Billy Rawlins. You might want to start there. Now, if you'll excuse me, I need to get back to my plans. Exercises have to be planned ready for the weekend." He turned, only to swivel back, again. "We miss her. We cared about her. I hope you find her murderer."

And that was it. They were dismissed.

PRIVATE WILLIAM RAWLINS sat in the adjutant's office, constantly looking about. There was a tremor in his hand, as he twirled a pencil round and round. He dropped the pencil twice, as a result.

Poor sod. Yvonne felt for him. He hardly presented as someone willing to assassinate anyone. Still, looks could be deceiving. She signalled for Tasha to take a seat next to her, before Simmonds grabbed it. Simmonds settled for a seat at right angles to both Rawlins and the DI.

Rawlins sneezed several times, and Yvonne reached into her pocket and took out a hanky. He accepted it, his face tense.

"You know why we're here, Billy?" the DI began.

"Staff said you're looking into Kate's death." Billy looked into her eyes. His own were red-rimmed, and in need of a good night's sleep.

"That's right, we are."

"Do you think I did it?"

"We're keeping an open mind. Did you?"

"No. I would never have hurt Kate. I told her not..." He looked sideways, at Simmonds, and fell silent.

Yvonne clenched her fists under the table and changed tack. "Billy, can I call you that?"

"Yes, ma'am."

"Do you know of anyone on the base with a smuggled, Kosovan-issue pistol?"

He looked surprised and shook his head.

"Were you aware of anyone with a grudge against Kate?"

He cocked his head to one side, looking at the ceiling. "Not specifically, no."

"Not specifically? What do you mean?"

"Just, no." He shook his head and his eyes darted to Simmonds again.

"You know," Yvonne leaned back in her chair, "I'm really thirsty. I could really do with a drink of water." She looked directly at Simmonds. "I'm not familiar with this base, could

I trouble you to fetch us some water, please?" She gave him a grimace, by way of apology.

He hesitated before roughly pushing back his chair with a loud scrape. "Certainly, I'll be right back." He said it like a warning, not to discuss stuff whilst he wasn't there.

As soon as he had gone, the DI leaned towards Billy. "What were you going to say? What was it, that you told her not to do?"

Billy also leaned in. "I told her not..." he flicked a look towards the door and licked his lips. "I told her not to meddle in those suicides." He bit his lip. "There are dark forces involved."

"Dark forces? What dark forces?"

Rawlins swallowed hard, and sat back in his chair. Simmonds was standing in the doorway.

"Do you have water, already?" The DI looked at Simmonds' empty hands.

"I've asked one of the lads to bring a jug and some glasses. Myself? I've requested coffee." He grinned, but his eyes were glass.

Yvonne felt hot dislike creeping through her. She wanted to shout at him at get out. She had been about to get somewhere. No use now. Billy Rawlins was sitting tight-lipped.

She put her hand in her pocket, gripping one of her cards. As soon as Simmonds got up to accept the drinks, from the young soldier who delivered them, Yvonne slipped it to Billy.

She thought at first he wasn't going to take it. But, with a glance towards the RMP officer, he palmed and then pocketed the card. The DI gave a nod to Tasha. She asked a few more questions. Routine. Then drank the water and rose, ready to leave. Simmonds was still sipping hot coffee. Billy headed out at the same time as Yvonne and Tasha.

The smell of aftershave was overwhelming.

"I'm here to help." Simmonds stood to his full height, glaring at Yvonne in the corridor, after Billy had left. "You're treating me like a parasite." He said the last through gritted teeth, saliva shards bursting forth with the words.

Yvonne wiped her chin. "Where's your colleague?" If he'd been expecting an apology, he was to be sorely disappointed.

"Thornton? He wasn't able to make it at such short notice. He had something else on."

"We have one more officer to interview today." The DI studied Simmonds' face. "Staff-Sergeant Jones. Do you want to be in on the interview?"

Simmonds looked at his watch. "It's getting on," he said, screwing up his face.

"Fine, we can discuss the interview with you another time. We'll go on ahead, without you."

She was surprised at Simmonds' lack of interest on the interview with Jones. She watched him leave, then turned to Tasha. "I can't work him out."

Tasha nodded. "It's hard to see what he can really add to the process and I think he knows it. He's angry because he's been ordered to be here."

"Billy didn't want to talk in front of him."

"That may just be because Simmonds is a symbol of army authority."

～

THEY FOUND Staff-Sergeant Jones talking to Forster, just as it was getting dark. Both were heading to their respective messes.

Forster acknowledged them with a wave, obviously content that they were getting on with it. As he walked away, Jones walked over to them.

He rubbed the faint stubble on his chin. In the lamp-light, Yvonne could clearly see his right hand knuckles were enlarged. She suspected he had done a lot of punching of people or things. She tried to get a look at his left, while Tasha began conversing with him. She didn't manage it.

"Is there somewhere we can go?" the DI asked, eventually. "We'd like to check a few things with you before heading off for the night."

"I can find us a quiet corner in the mess," he offered. "There won't be more than a few NCO's in there, anyway."

"That'll be fine." She nodded and checked her watch. It was nine o'clock. She and Tasha had eaten nothing since lunchtime, and nothing decent, even then. She was grateful when he suggested they all eat in the mess.

"I'll get food ordered. I'll see you in there." With that, he was gone to organise food, leaving Yvonne and Tasha to attempt to get into the mess without an NCO with them.

"Will we get in?" Tasha hesitated outside the door.

"Let's at least try." Yvonne palmed her warrant card, in case she needed it.

She needn't have worried. The young man from behind the bar, whom she had seen on a previous occasion, let them in without even checking their ID. He was satisfied he'd seen her with Sergeant Callaghan.

They were sipping sparkling water, when Staff-Sergeant Jones arrived back with a tray of sandwiches. "Sorry it's not hot food." His smile appeared forced. "Things are still not back to normal. They won't be until the New Year."

"Not a problem, thank you for this." Yvonne was just happy to have something to eat. She picked up a tuna triangle and flicked through her notes. "Staff Sergeant Jones-"

"Call me Staff. Everyone does."

"Staff. Where were you the night Steven Whyte was killed?"

He looked like he'd been slapped. He paused, mouth open, before answering with a question. "I thought this was supposed to be about Kate Nilsson?" he said, crossing his arms and sitting back in his chair.

"It is." Yvonne smiled by way of apology. "But, the two deaths may be linked, and I'm just trying to place everybody. I *will* ask the same question of others. I'd also like to know where you were when Kate Nilsson was murdered."

"What did Stephen Whyte say to you?" His eyes were half-lidded.

The DI flicked her own up from her notes. There was silence for a second or two, then, "Why do you ask that? Are you afraid of what he might have told me?" She didn't move her gaze from his.

He huffed. "Well, something's made you suspect me of murdering my own soldiers. Why would I do that? Give me one reason."

"I'm not saying you did. But, since you ask, I don't know...perhaps they saw something in Iraq or Afghanistan, that you would rather they hadn't, or that you wanted to cover up."

He shifted in his seat and looked towards the glass doors. "That's pretty fantastical thinking."

The DI thought she detected a faint flush of colour in

his tanned face. "Do you mean nothing bad happened? Or that you wouldn't try covering it up?"

He locked eyes with her. "If you're talking about me, both apply."

"What about anyone else?"

"If anyone else had anything to hide, I didn't hear of it."

"So, you can't think of any reason why those two soldiers would be cut down in cold blood, back on civvy street?"

"Have you considered terrorism?"

"We have. It's a way down the list, however, and no-one has claimed responsibility."

"I see."

"I'm sorry, Staff, you still haven't answered my question."

"I was in my quarters, watching television and getting an early night, when Stephen was killed."

"Can anyone verify that?"

"No. I mean, not likely."

"What about when Kate was killed?"

"I may have been out in Chester. No. No, wait a minute. I was in my quarters then, as well. I had the day off, athough I was still here at the base. I'm due to go on leave next week."

Yvonne noted the lack of alibi in her notes.

"Listen, I don't care what you think. I didn't kill those two, decent soldiers. Neither did I have a hand in it."

"Do you know who did?"

"No, Inspector. I do not." He emphasised each word, as though to underline the fact and convince her to look elsewhere.

Yvonne glanced at Tasha, who was quietly munching on a sandwich, observing and saying nothing.

"How well did you know Kate?"

"I knew her as an officer knows their soldiers. There was nothing inappropriate, if that's what you're suggesting."

"I'm sorry, I wasn't suggesting anything. Forgive me, I have to ask these questions."

He grunted, and a frown creased his forehead.

"Are you aware of anyone else having a close relationship with her?"

"Only Wayne. Private Hedges. And that was only as close friends. As far as I am aware, there was nothing romantic between those two. Oh, there was banter, sure. A few of the lads would make the odd remark and cheeky wolf-whistle but, otherwise? Kate wasn't romantically involved."

"What about Private Rawlins?"

"Schoolboy crush. Knew he wasn't going to get anywhere and, as far as I know, was resigned to that fact."

"So, Kate knew of his crush on her?"

"She couldn't miss it. None of us could."

"How did she reject him?"

"She wasn't unkind with it, if that's what you're thinking. Kate had a knack for letting people down gently. She knew how to smooth things over. I'm not saying it's impossible, but I doubt her death was over some failed romantic triste."

"I'm inclined to think you're right." Yvonne nodded.

Staff Jones took a long swig of his pint, a moustache of froth lingered on his upper lip, until he licked it off. "Anything else I can help you with?"

"Maybe. Who had or has access to Kate's barrack room?"

"No-one."

"Really?"

"Really. Ever since her death, it's been closed, except for yourself and SIB. At some point soon, it will be cleared and her things sent home to her parents."

"Who authorises that?"

"The Major-General."

"Broderick Forster?"

"Him and SIB, yes."

"I see. Anyone else have keys?"

"All keys are in Forster's office. The room is locked when he's not in there."

Yvonne brushed the crumbs from her lap. "Well, I think that is pretty much everything, for now. Thank you, Staff, for speaking to us. I know your time is precious."

"It's a murder investigation, Inspector." He shrugged. "Of course I'd speak to you."

ON THE JOURNEY back to Newtown, Yvonne was quiet. Tasha broke the silence after about twenty minutes. "He seemed genuine, when he talked about Kate, didn't he? I didn't detect signs of lying." The psychologist paused, making a right turn. "However, there were times he pulled back. Got defensive."

"Like when I asked him if anything untoward had happened in Iraq or Afghanistan."

"It looked like it got him thinking. Sparked something off."

"Like he knows something."

"Or suspects someone."

"Well, if he does, he's not telling us."

Be interesting to know what he does next. Shame we couldn't stay on the base."

"I keep coming back to what Stephen Whyte said. Start with Jones and Callaghan and work up. He was convinced someone high-up was behind Kate's death."

Tasha pursed her lips. "If it's murder to cover up something, then the information or the event must be pretty explosive."

"Could we be looking at torture of prisoners, I wonder?

Or unlawful killing? Stories like that hit the headlines every now and then."

"And careers are ruined."

"Exactly. But if that's what we're looking at here, and Stephen was correct, then the cover-up went pretty high up the food chain."

"Forster?"

Yvonne pulled a face. "I just don't see that. I don't get that sort of vibe about him."

"Psychopaths are often charming." Tasha glanced at her friend.

"I know. I know." The DI sighed. "I'm keeping an open mind, Tasha. I want to go back to Kate's things. Her photos and stuff. I'll speak to Llewellyn and see if we can bag some of it up as evidence and study it at at the station."

"Do you think Forster and SIB will let you do that?"

"Sure, why not. I'll go through those photos with a fine tooth comb. I *have* to know what she was on to."

"Another hour and we'll be back."

Yvonne sat upright. "Oh God, you've got that drive to your house after that. Stay at mine. It'll take minutes to get the spare room ready and you can drive up to your cottage tomorrow morning."

"That would be great. But, if you need some help convincing Llewellyn, I'll be happy to hang around until lunchtime."

Yvonne grinned broadly. "It's no bloody wonder you're my best friend." And, within ten minutes, she had fallen asleep.

Tasha chuckled to herself. "I'll try not to take that personally," she said, to no-one in particular. She finished the drive back to Newtown in silence.

14

INTERFERENCE FROM ABOVE

The DCI looked up from his paperwork, as Yvonne knocked and entered.

"How did it go yesterday?" he asked, his eyes wandering her face, his voice soft.

"Like wading through treacle."

"Sit down, please." Yvonne did as she was told.

"What do you mean, like treacle? Do you mean they aren't cooperating?"

"No, I don't mean that. They are cooperating, to a degree. It's just..." She turned her gaze to the window. "There are things they are not saying."

"Who's not saying what?"

"Everyone in this investigation." She stopped her thousand-yard stare and brought her eyes back to his. "I feel like everyone is holding something back. And that goes for both army and civilians."

Llewellyn sat back in his chair, his gaze soft and steady.

"I've been asked to pull you off the base." He sighed and ran a hand through his hair.

The DI noticed he had a little more grey at his temples.

She sat forward, fixing him with a fierce stare. "What do you mean, pull me off the base? You mean stop me going to Dale?"

"Yes."

"What? Why now? Have I touched a raw nerve? Who asked you to pull me off?"

Llewellyn sighed. "The Chief Super."

Yvonne froze, her mouth half-open. "Why would he do that?"

"You were only supposed to be going there once or twice, remember?"

"But, I've just started getting somewhere." She put a hand either side of her head, as though to shut out what he was telling her.

"I thought you said it was like wading through treacle, anyway? Concentrate on the crime scene and the weapon used. More villagers should be questioned, those around Llydiart."

"Uniform can do that." Yvonne gave him a defiant look.

"I'm sorry, I've had my orders." Llewellyn's face was flushed, his eyes downcast.

"They got to him, didn't they? I'll bet this is Forster's doing, on the behest of his NCOs."

Llewellyn shook his head. "I doubt it was Forster. He would have come to me, direct."

"Then, who? Who would want my investigation to flounder?"

"Yvonne, that's a bit dramatic, isn't it? Like I said, you can continue with the crime scene. I'm not taking you off the case."

"What about Stephen Whyte?"

"Who?"

"Corporal Whyte. What about his death? I'm convinced

it's linked. Someone is following my progress on this investigation."

Llewellyn picked up his ball-point, clicking the top in and out. "Cheshire are investigating Whyte's death. What else can you do at the base? What would you want to do?"

"I want to go through Kate's things, again. Before her barrack room is cleared. She'd been gathering evidence of wrong-doing, I'm sure of it."

"Okay. Okay. I'll speak to Forster."

"Thank you, sir. Can I ask another favour?" The DI rose from her chair.

"Go on."

"Can you find out, from the chief super, who it was that requested I not go back to the base?"

He nodded. "I'll try, but if it's someone from the MOD, then-"

"I know, shadowy figures. But please try."

Tasha was waiting with Dewi in the coffee area, when Yvonne returned. Tasha supressed a giggle at the size of the DI's scowl.

"What's up?" Dewi asked, blowing air through tight lips.

"We keep going. We've obviously got someone rattled."

"You wanted to look at Kate's photos again." Tasha blew on her hot coffee, not quite sure how to react to Yvonne's mood.

"Llewellyn is talking to Forster, trying to get permission for us to access her room one last time." Yvonne looked at her friend. "Do you need to get back to the cottage?"

"I do, for now, but I can be back again tomorrow. If I can be of any use."

"That would be great." Yvonne's scowl dissipated and

she even managed a grin. "Dewi and I are hoping to go back to Dale tomorrow. Would be good if you could come with us."

They cleared away their mugs and were about to get on when the DCI strode in, looking sheepish. "I'm sorry." He drew alongside the DI and rubbed his chin, as though searching for the right words. "Kate's barrack room has been cleared, Yvonne."

"What?"

"The room has been cleaned, ready for a new occupant."

"But we hadn't finished."

"I'm sorry. But you know the room itself wasn't a crime scene. They couldn't keep it like that forever."

"But she hasn't even been gone two weeks. I made it clear I hadn't finished."

"It's not a shrine, Yvonne. Look, I know you're disappointed. Forster said to give you his apologies."

"Well, they'll help solve the case, of course."

The DCI sighed, frustration clouding his features. "I'd like your interim report by the end of the week," was all he said, before turning on his heel and heading down the corridor.

"What now?" Dewi pouted, tucking his chair under the table.

"We go to Kate's parents. Seek their permission to go through whatever the army returned to them."

"Righty-oh. We'd better make a move then."

"I'll see you tomorrow." Tasha gave the DI's hand a squeeze. "I hope you find what you're looking for."

～

SOMEONE HAD CLEANED Lars and Hayley's home to the point of obsession. All traces of Christmas were gone. The glass and metal shone and all wood surfaces smelled strongly of polish. Not a speck of dust could be seen anywhere.

Lars had let them in before he left the house. Yvonne and Dewi took off their shoes in the hall. Even so, the DI worried in case she caused a mess somehow.

Hayley came to see them, still wearing an apron and rubber gloves. Eyes puffy, looking in need of a good sleep, she pulled two chairs out for them in the kitchen.

"How are you doing?" Yvonne's question was almost a whisper.

Hayley's eyes searched her face, as though to check if the DI was truly looking for an answer, or merely asking to be polite. "I'm existing, Inspector. I'm getting through the days any way I can. I loved her from the moment she was an extra line on my pregnancy test." Hayley looked away to the window. "I can still feel her little head on my shoulder and smell her sweet baby hair. I nursed her through sickness, injury and disappointments. I cheered with her through all her triumphs. My baby. My baby girl. I'm a mom. It's who I am. It's who I've been since I first held her in my arms. I feel lost. I am lost. But I can still feel her cuddled against my chest." Hayley looked back at the DI.

Yvonne nodded. "Those memories are so precious. That's a part of her you'll always have."

"Have you found her killer?" Hayley interjected. "I need that. That's what's keeping me sane: the thought that her killer will soon be found and punished."

Yvonne exchanged glances with Dewi. "That's what we're here to talk about, Mrs Nilsson. We understand the army have returned some of her things."

Hayley turned to fill a kettle. She put it on the stand,

switched it on, and turned her attention back to the detectives. "We got a box back from them yesterday. I haven't opened it, yet. I haven't felt ready."

Yvonne nodded her understanding. "May we look inside the box, Mrs Nilsson?"

Hayley leaned her head to one side. "Do you think there's something in there that will help you?"

The DI rubbed her chin. "I think there could be, yes."

"Then go ahead. Whatever helps."

"Thank you." Dewi held the cupboard door open for Hayley, as she removed cups from it. She hadn't asked them if they wanted tea. She just needed to do something.

Yvonne understood this and accepted her cup in that spirit. Ten minutes later, she and Dewi were climbing the stairs.

"Where did Lars go?" Dewi asked, in hushed tones, once they were inside Kate's bedroom.

Yvonne didn't answer, she was taking in the fact that Kate's was the only room to have escaped the obsessive cleaning. Again, this was no surprise to her. She felt tears prick her eyelids. "Let's not interfere with anything except the box," she said to Dewi.

In the box were a few books, the wall photographs, trinkets, jewellery and perfume. Eclectic stuff from Kate's barrack-room drawers and boxes.

Yvonne hunted for the photo she had looked at with Tasha - the one showing Kate, Wayne Hedges and Stephen Whyte at the James Bond Casino night. She found it almost at the bottom of the box.

Smiling faces. Smart, beautiful clothes. Happiness. Behind Kate, was a giant card, the ace of hearts. On the table, an open bottle of champagne. The three of them appeared merry. There was nothing else that stood out. And yet, Tasha had felt sure there may be significance to the photo, due to its positioning in the ones Kate had taken of her room.

She turned the frame over. The card in the back was held in with tape. She looked up at Dewi, a warning of what she was about to do, and began peeling back the tape.

Dewi shot a glance towards the door, before his eyes came back to what Yvonne was doing.

Although she felt guilt about the intrusion, the DI's curiosity drove her on. The tape came off with relative ease and she gently teased the back out of the frame. Under-neath, was a sheet of paper - one that would have been with the frame when it was purchased. She lifted it. A torn piece of notepaper floated to the floor. She rushed down to grab it, almost bumping heads with Dewi, who'd had the same urge.

Inside the frame, was a small photograph of three teenagers. They were roughly thirteen to fourteen years old. The picture reminded her of another she'd seen in Kate's room. The one of Kate, Wayne and Stephen on a street somewhere, a large cafe-restaurant in the background. The photograph she was holding was perhaps older, judging by the cars parked along the street.

Dewi handed her the paper which he had beaten her to. "Helen Reynolds, Scotty McEwan and Tom Rendon, 2003.'

Yvonne looked at Dewi. "This is a photo of the three soldiers whose deaths Kate was investigating. The three suspicious deaths."

"I know. I'd been wondering why Kate had chosen those particular deaths to investigate. She obviously felt there was a connection."

"So, they were friends as children. Long before they joined the army."

"Right. Are you thinking what I'm thinking?"

"That we ought to look into their childhood backgrounds?"

"Exactly." Yvonne nodded vigorously.

"But not tell Llewellyn." Dewi pulled a face.

"Not yet, no."

"There's something else." Dewi pointed to an underlined name, on the other side of the torn paper. T.H. Davis. This was in the same writing as the names on the front. It looked like Kate's hand, judging by the writings they had seen in her room.

The letters in the name appeared thick and uneven, as though someone, presumably Kate, had drawn and redrawn them - doodling. Perhaps, deep in thought.

"Who's T.H. Davis?" Yvonne frowned. The new name confused things.

"Maybe another soldier who died?"

"Or another soldier she suspected." She placed the small photo and paper on the bed. "Let's fix this frame back together. We'll keep the hidden inserts and take them with us."

"Damn, I should have brought an evidence bag in from the car.' Dewi tutted at his forgetfulness.

"It's okay." Yvonne pulled one out of her pocket. "I'm not sealing it up just yet. I need to think. We've got to go back to Dale. Speak to Forster."

Dewi wrinkled his nose. "Llewellyn's going to love that."

"You're right." Yvonne paused at the door. "I'll speak to Thornton. Ask if SIB know who T.H.Davis is. If he's on the base, or an ex-soldier, they should be able to trace him."

"And if he's dead, which I hope he's not," Dewi added swiftly, "then that probably makes him even easier to trace."

There was one more photo the DI wished to take with

her, and that was the one of Kate, Wayne and Stephen. The one taken in what appeared to be the same street as the hidden photograph. She quickly found it amongst Kate's things, and placed everything else back as she had located it. "Come on, Dewi. We've got work to do," she said, before exiting down the stairs.

"YOU WANT ME TO WHAT?" Thornton's voice boomed down the phone.

"I'd like you to help us trace T. H. Davis. We think he might be a soldier on the base. Or maybe an ex-soldier. Can you help us?" Yvonne bit her lip, half-expecting Thornton to decline. There was an agonising few seconds silence.

"Okay, I'll help you. How far do you want me to go back?"

"The late nineties should do it. Alive or dead, I need to know.'

"What are you up to?"

"It's just one of the lines of our enquiry," she said simply.

"This person a suspect in Kate Nilsson's murder?"

"Possibly." Yvonne cleared her throat. "Could I ask you to keep that thought to yourself for now?"

"Understood. Why?"

"The last person who helped me was murdered." She said it for pure devilment. Thornton grunted on the other end but he didn't question further.

FOLLOWING THE CALL, she turned to her DS. "Dewi, we should speak to Sam Walters again, about Helen Reynolds."

"Find out about about her life as a teenager?"

"And her connection to Scotty and Tom, when she was young."

"I'll fetch our coats."

Yvonne fumbled in her jacket pockets for her car keys. "I have an idea."

"Oh, yeah?"

"It's something Scotty's father, Gordon McEwan, said to me when I interviewed him last time. He said Scotty had grown up in care homes and foster care."

"So you're wondering if that's how they came to know each other?"

"Could be worth asking. Sam would most likely know if Helen had spent time in care."

"Let's go." Dewi finished getting his coat on and they headed out the door.

THERE WAS a lot more happening on the site, as they entered the Newtown bypass works. Yvonne made her way to the office in search of Sam Walters while Dewi parked the car and then played catch-up. She was glad of her wellingtons.

He was taller than she remembered. He looked at her as though speaking to her was the last thing he needed at that moment.

She slowed her pace as she got closer, and saw his disappointment.

"I'm sorry." She grimaced. "Is it all right to talk to you now?

"Well I..." He looked down at her muddy wellingtons and crumpled skirt. His face softened. "All right. Will it take long? Only, I'm expecting a delivery of slabs any time now and we're on a deadline."

Yvonne shook her head, just as Dewi got to them. "It won't take long."

Sam led them over to the pre-fab office. He climbed the steps and creaked the door open. "So, how can I help?"

Yvonne took out her notebook. "I wanted to ask a couple more questions abut Helen." Her pen refused to work. She sucked the end and tried again, circling the tip round and round on the paper, desperate for it to respond, to no avail.

Sam took one off his desk and handed it to her. "Here," he said, between clenched teeth.

She took it and thanked him, feeling awkward.

"What was it you wanted to know?"

Yvonne cleared her throat. "Sam, did Helen ever discuss her childhood with you?"

"Err, yes. I guess she did. Once or twice."

"Can you remember what she said?"

He blew out a puff of air, while he thought about it. "You know, I can't really remember that much. She grew up in North Wales. Was an only child."

"An only child?" Yvonne felt a knot of disappointment develop in her stomach. "She had a family, then?"

"She told me she remembered her mum but not really her dad. I think he left, not long after she was born. He didn't return. She couldn't remember anything about him."

"I see. What about her mum? Were they close?"

"Very. But her mum passed away when Helen was six years old."

Out of the corner of her eye, Yvonne saw Dewi move forward to the edge of his seat. "What happened to Helen? Did she go to relatives after her mum passed away?"

"Not that I remember, no. She went into care, I think."

The DI paused in her note-taking. "Can you remember where she was, when she was in care, Sam?"

"No. No, I can't remember. I know she was in a care home for a few years before going into foster care."

"Did she ever talk to you about friends she made in care?"

"She did, yes. In fact, she'd stayed friends with a few of them. They made a pact to enlist together. They played war games together as kids."

"So, they enlisted together?"

"They did, and they remained best buddies."

"Do you remember who the friends were?" Yvonne exchanged glances with Dewi.

"I remember one of her best friends being Scotty. She was devastated when he killed himself."

"You knew about that?"

"Well, yes. He hung himself after a few drinks."

"Did you ever doubt that he killed himself?"

"Not really. Well, I had no reason to doubt it."

"What about Helen? Did she doubt it?"

"She was gutted. I remember her being hurt, disappointed and angry. She didn't want to believe it. She wanted to believe that he'd have talked to her, first. She'd been pretty vocal in her suspicion that he had been attacked."

"Did she say who she thought might have attacked him?"

"Not that made any sense. I mean, she pointed the finger at a few people. She probably ought to have been disciplined, but everyone understood she ranting because she was in pain. His loss hit her hard. Actually, that was probably one of the only times when she wasn't harshly disciplined for something."

"Can you remember the names of the other childhood friends?"

"Tom. Can't remember his other name. And Stephen

Whyte. There may have been others. I don't recall. We only dated for a couple of years. I doubt she told me everything in that time."

"How old was she when she enlisted?"

"Seventeen."

"Do you know where she was, when she was in care? I mean, where she was in North Wales?"

"Wrexham. She was from Wrexham. Her mum passed away in Wrexham hospital." Sam stood up. "I'm sorry, officers, but I really have to get on. I can see the lorry drawing up with part of my load on it. I've got to check it and sign it in. The lads can't start the next phase until we've unloaded it."

"Of course." Yvonne nodded. "We've taken up enough of your time."

Just as she got to the door, she turned swiftly on her heel, to face him again. "So sorry, one last thing. Does the name T.H. Davis mean anything to you?"

Sam looked at her blankly and shrugged. "Sorry."

"No matter. Thank you, Mr Walters. You've been enormously helpful."

Yvonne's mood had picked up. "Okay, Dewi. We have a connection between these soldiers."

"Yeah, we now know how and why they became such good friends, and it pre-dated the army."

"It did. The question is, what did they know that put them all at risk?"

"Are you still thinking something happened out in the field?"

"It's a possibility. We still have the personnel files. I say we go over them again. Look at all the places they toured.

The weapon used to kill Kate came from Bosnia. Perhaps we should start there."

"Right you are, ma'am."

HARRY THORNTON WAS deep in conversation with DCI Llewellyn when they arrived back in the station.

"I need to take a leak," Dewi announced out loud. Thornton and Llewellyn stopped what they were doing and looked at the two detectives.

"Ah, Inspector Giles. Just the person I've been looking for." Thornton gave Llewellyn a pat on the arm and headed over to the DI. "Shall we go get a coffee?"

She followed him through to the coffee area, feeling wary.

"Been anywhere interesting?" he asked, and she again felt crumpled and dog-eared in his presence. Even the knot of his well-chosen tie was perfect.

She, in comparison, had mud splashed up her stockings, damp creases in her shirt, and a coffee stain on her blouse. He was looking at it.

She eyed him coolly, choosing not to answer his question.

"Look," he hissed, grabbing her by the arm and closing the door behind her. "Stop with all this us-and-them bull-shit. I'm not competing with you. We're not hiding anything from you. We had nothing to do with Corporal Whyte's death."

Yvonne stood, wide-eyed at the outburst.

He continued, "Do you think it's easy for us? You know they call us 'the feds'. That's the name the sappers call us. Their mouths are tighter than a ducks arse, the minute we come on the scene. Closed ranks, disappearing paperwork, we've seen the lot." His eyes relaxed a little. "Look, I want to know who killed Kate Nilsson and Stephen Whyte as much as you do." He appeared deflated, like all the fight had suddenly left him.

Yvonne could feel the heat in her cheeks. She felt guilty for upsetting him and shutting him out. "I'm sorry, Harry. Sometimes in this job it's hard to know who to trust."

"I get that." He let go of her arm. "Most people see the army as one cohesive unit. They don't see the internal struggles and conflicting needs within it."

"Tea?" Yvonne looked towards the kettle.

"Please." He nodded and a smile brightened his face. "Let you have both barrels then, didn't I?"

The DI laughed, with genuine warmth. "You certainly did, Harold Thornton."

With hot teas going down nicely, he pulled a face. "I'm afraid I have some bad news for you."

"You haven't found T.H.Davis?"

"No. Sorry. We found a T.L.Davis and a J.H.Davis. We found a fair few Davises, actually, but not the one you're looking for."

Yvonne believed him. "It's okay." She sighed. "It was a long shot. Kate had written the name down. It was among some things at her parents. Thing is, she gave no clue as to why she had written it. I just thought it might be a soldier."

"Yeah, well, we checked present and ex-army records, and no-one."

I guess it'll remain a mystery, for now, but thank you for checking. I *do* appreciate it."

"You're welcome."

Dewi joined them for a brew and Yvonne relaxed more

than she had in a while. The air had needed clearing and she was glad it was done.

AFTER THE TEA, Yvonne found her bag and checked her phone. She had three missed calls. She didn't recognise the number but tried ringing it. She got the voicemail of Billy Rawlins and left a message to say she was sorry she'd missed him and could he please call her back when he got the message. She left the phone on her desk all afternoon, but there were no further calls from him.

15

MAKING CONNECTIONS

Yvonne and Tasha had agreed to meet at their favourite talking shop, 'The Bank' tea rooms, in Newtown.

The DI had been waiting a good fifteen minutes, by the time her friend arrived, and was already studying the photographs found in Kate's room.

The two most important were the ones of Kate, Wayne and Stephen together, and the older one of Scotty, Helen and Tom. She placed them next to each other, flicking her gaze between them.

The pictures shared similarities, from the poses of the two guys and one girl, to the objects in the street behind them. They were taken maybe fifteen years apart. That was evident from the cars, parked along the street. There were a few minor changes in the scenery, but there was no doubting it was the same street, and almost exactly the same spot.

She took out her notebook and flicked through her interview notes from everyone she had talked to in connection with the case. She was in the middle of this, when Tasha rushed in, sporting a big grin.

"What are we having, then?" Tasha plopped her bag and coat onto one chair, and herself on another.

"Homity pie and strong apple tea." Yvonne grinned back. "Thought you might be late, so I started working."

"Yeah. Sorry about that. Traffic was heavier than usual today. Extra disruption from the bypass works. So, you've been busy, then." Tasha nodded towards the notes and photos in front of the DI.

"Take a look at these pictures." Yvonne placed the two of interest in front of her friend.

"Oh, yes." Tasha placed them side-by-side. "Two sets of friends, years apart. Five of the six are now dead." She looked up at the Yvonne, both deadly serious at the implications.

"We ought to warn Forster and get some protection put in place for Wayne Hedges." Yvonne pursed her lips.

Tasha nodded. "So, am I looking for anything else in these?"

"Look at the background, Tasha."

It didn't take too long. "We're looking at the same street, just a different time."

"Right. These two photographs were taken in the same spot. My question is why? And is it significant?"

Tasha peered more closely at the photo which included Kate. "You know, these three look like they are celebrating something."

"I would like to speak to Wayne again, and find out where these photos were taken. I've got a feeling they were taken in Wrexham."

"Oh?" Tasha raised her eyebrows. "What makes you say that?"

"Well," Yvonne checked her notes, "Gordon McEwan told me Scotty grew up in Wrexham. The care homes were there, and so, too, his foster carers. Sam Walters told me Helen Reynolds grew up in Wrexham - also in care homes and foster care."

Tasha pointed. "There's part of a sign in these photos on the restaurant, in the background. Maybe we can use Google's 'Up My Street' to try to find it."

"What's wrong with visiting Wrexham? And how did you know I'd want to see the street?"

"I know you." Tasha laughed. "But, I agree. There's something about those two photographs being eerily similar. It suggests the second one was taken in that spot by design."

"Agreed." Yvonne flicked to another page in her notebook. "I have a name for the children's home. It was called Sunnymede. See the partial sign?"

"Oh, I see what you're suggesting. They could perhaps be outside Sunnymede children's home."

"Just a thought. Maybe after lunch, we should go back to the station and Google Sunnymede and find out. A tour around with 'Up My Street', could tell us if we're on the right track."

"Wow." Tasha sat back in her chair. "I should be late for our meetings more often."

The homity pie and apple teas were delivered to the table and they said relatively little as they finished them. Both were lost in their own thoughts about the dead youngsters in the photographs.

≈

THE DCI WAS WAITING for Yvonne when she got back. "Can I have a word?" He appeared stressed and she bit her lip.

Tasha slunk out and went to find Dewi.

"Yvonne, Private Billy Rawlins has gone missing from Dale Barracks. He's AWOL."

"AWOL? Seriously? Oh no." She frowned. "Well, we've got to find him."

"Cheshire Police are looking into the disappearance but they want to know what we know."

"They want our help?"

"Not exactly. They want to know what *you* know about the disappearance."

"What I know? Well, I know nothing. I didn't know he was going to disappear, if that's what you're suggesting."

"Apparently, yours was the last number he tried to ring, before he disappeared. He tried you several times, apparently. Did you speak to him?"

"No. No, I didn't. But, that's right." Yvonne was remembering the missed calls. "I had three missed calls on my phone. At the time, I didn't know who they were from, but I rang the number back and got his voicemail message. I left a message for him to try me again. I kept my phone on all afternoon, but he didn't call."

"I see." Llewellyn paced over to the window. "Maybe he killed Private Nilsson and Corporal Whyte. Perhaps he wanted to confess to you but changed his mind and legged it."

"I don't think so, sir."

"No?"

"I just don't see Billy as someone who could run down and assassinate Kate or Stephen. Anyway, he loved Kate."

"Well, stalkers do kill."

"I don't think he was stalking her, sir."

"Even so. He is now a person of extreme interest, both to the military police and to Cheshire Police. He has also become our number one suspect in the murder of Kate Nilsson."

"Wait." Yvonne strode over to Llewellyn. "How did they know he phoned me? Did they get the phone records already?"

"Not yet. His phone was left in his room. The lights were on and the door had been left wide open. Like he'd left in a hurry."

"Did he have his wallet with him?"

"Yes. He had money and a small rucksack. They think he took his bedroll with him too."

"But he left his phone."

"Yes."

"Seems odd."

"A phone would make him easier to trace. I think he probably left his phone behind so he couldn't be found." Llewellyn folded his arms.

YVONNE NEEDED TIME. Time to get her head around this latest development. She didn't believe for one minute that Billy was the killer of Kate and Stephen. So why, then, had he gone missing? She felt a sinking feeling in the pit of her stomach. She left Llewellyn and went in search of Dewi and Tasha.

"I think Billy Rawlins might be in danger," she announced, as she found them chatting in the corridor.

She filled them in with what the DCI had told her. Then added, "Llewellyn's got him pegged as the number one suspect."

"Well, I can understand why..." Dewi leaned his head on one side. "You would, wouldn't you?"

Yvonne shook her head and looked towards Tasha. "Tasha, you were there when I interviewed Billy. What did you think? Oh, and he tried to call me yesterday. He tried three times and then left his phone behind in his room."

Tasha narrowed her eyes, looking down at the floor for what seemed like an age. "I'm inclined to agree with you, Yvonne. I think it unlikely that Billy is our killer. I know he's a soldier, but hunting down his own? I can't see it. I think he'd struggle even to kill the enemy out in the field. But we shouldn't completely discount the idea. If found, he should be approached with caution."

DEWI FIRED UP HIS LAPTOP, Yvonne drumming her fingers on the back of his chair. Tasha had zoned out, deep in thought, behind them.

"Come on. Come on." Dewi frowned at the rotating symbol in the centre of the screen. "Damn wifi."

As soon as Google came up, Dewi typed in 'Sunnymede, Wrexham'. The result ran over a number of pages. Still on the first page, Yvonne gave Tasha a poke. "That's it."

"You're sure that's the one?" Tasha scratched her head. "I thought you said it was a children's home?"

"And this is a hotel and restaurant." Yvonne nodded. "You're right. Perhaps we should keep looking."

Dewi clicked on every link on the first three pages. After that, the suggestions were way off anything they were looking for. He stopped clicking and turned to his two companions. "Still coming back to the hotel and restaurant as the nearest match."

"Okay. Well, let's click further into that one and see what comes up. Maybe it used to be a children's home."

They found a link on the homepage, titled 'History', and clicked on it.

"Wow." Yvonne put her hand through her hair. "Bingo."

Dewi read out loud: "Began as an orphanage in the Victorian era and became a children's home in the fifties." Dewi got up from the chair to allow Yvonne to read in more depth.

"Looks like this is definitely the Sunnymede we're after." She frowned. "But the reunions." She looked disappointed. "I felt sure those two photographs were taken at some sort of reunion." She clicked back to the homepage. "That sign. The first part of it is definitely the one from the photographs."

Tasha leaned back against the desk. "Well, it's a hotel and restaurant. Doesn't it make sense that they might meet up there? It didn't need to have been organised at the children's home. Particularly if that home no longer exists as a home."

"You're right, of course. All I meant was, if it's no longer a children's home, all records will likely have gone."

"Why don't we go along to the place and ask? If there were reunions, the owners would most likely know." Dewi raised his brows and shrugged. "They may be able to confirm with us the names of people who attended."

"T.H.Davis." Yvonne's eyes shone. "I wonder…"

THE JOURNEY to Wrexham was a lot more smooth than they'd anticipated. Once there, and with the sat nav, they found their destination easily. Parking, however, was a different matter and, if they had had a swear box on board, Dewi would have been broke.

He had a distinctly dishevelled look, as they got out of the car, his tie angled sideways, his shirt crumpled. The temperature dictated they wear big coats, saving his pride. Yvonne smiled to herself.

Tasha waited for them in the car.

The hotel had been painted recently. It stood out from the more bedraggled looking buildings next to it. It had the appearance of being well-cared for. A neat and symmetrical garden led to a similarly neat and well-balanced frontage. The sign next to the door boasted four stars. The front door was bounded by a large porch, with a freshly-painted, gold lattice-work top.

A tall man in his late-thirties met them in the lobby. "Mark Aston." He gave both officers a firm handshake. "Come on in."

Off to her right, Yvonne could see the glass-fronted entrance to the lobby. She'd recognised the outside as that in Kate's photographs, and was now scanning the restaurant to see if she could locate where the inside photos were taken.

A female diner gave her a stern look and the DI turned her attention back to Mark Aston. She was surprised to find his grey-blue eyes on her.

Dewi was deeply engaged in informing Mark of their reasons for being there. She rubbed the scar on her chin, suddenly conscious of it. Her skin flushed. She cleared her throat, noisily. "Thanks for seeing us, Mark. I realise you're running a busy hotel here." She could hear the constant clatter and voices from the restaurant, and both staff and guests wandered to and fro, as she spoke. "Is there some-where we can go?"

"Oh, yes. Of course." He appeared to come to, as though having been away in his thoughts for a while. He ran a hand over his forehead and on through his light-brown hair, his brow furrowed. "Let's go into the office. We'll be able to hear ourselves think in there."

It was a well-ordered office. The DI was impressed. The whole place, so far, appeared to be run efficiently. Staff appeared focussed and competent.

"How long have you managed the hotel?" She pulled out her notebook.

"Seven years." He smiled. "I took over from my father, when he became too ill to run it himself."

"Your father's ill? I'm sorry."

He grimaced. "Dementia. It's a helluva thing."

Yvonne nodded. "It looks to me like you're doing a great job." She smiled, shifting her weight between feet.

"Oh, please...sit down." He pulled out a couple of chairs for them and then pulled out his own from behind his desk. "It took me a couple of years to fully get into the swing of things and to earn the staff's trust. But, yes, I hope I'm living up to my father's legacy."

The DI glanced towards the sash window. "Can I ask when this became a hotel?"

"Er, sure. It was 1999. There'd been a children's home here for decades. My father had always thought it would make a fantastic hotel and restaurant. It was his big vision. He convinced my mother they should buy it, when the home closed."

"I see. Is your mother still involved?"

"She passed away."

"Oh, I'm sorry. Forgive me, I-"

"It's okay. It's been ten years now. I still miss her, but it's no longer raw." He shrugged.

"Do you know why the home closed?" Dewi was taking his own notes, his head bent over as he asked the question.

"There was a scandal. I don't know all the ins and outs, but it centred around alleged sexual abuse."

"Of the children?"

Mark nodded. "There was an investigation. My father said only one or two people were prosecuted in the end, even though a massive pedophile ring was rumoured to have taken advantage of the youngsters here. It was a major news item that appeared to go nowhere in the end. The guy who ran the home ended up in jail."

"Who was that?" Yvonne paused her writing, her blue eyes intent on what Mark had to say.

"Oh God, erm...somebody Broadman. Tim Broadman?" He screwed up his face, looking at the ceiling.

"Not T.H.Davis?"

"T.H. Davis? No, definitely not T.H.Davis. He got away clean. They decided he hadn't been involved, even though he'd been described by some of the kids." He had both Yvonne and Dewi's undivided attention. He gave them a look, as if to say 'What have I said?'

"Who *is* T.H.Davis?" Yvonne's voice was low and firm.

"Well, he was the local MP. At the time of the scandal, he was into his third term of office."

"Your knowledge is very good." The DI pressed her pen to her lips, pensive.

"My father kept cuttings. It was all part of the history of the place."

Yvonne nodded. "Of course. Do you still have those cuttings?"

"Probably. Somewhere." He put his hand over his mouth, his eyes moving side-to-side, as though trying to remember. "I'm not sure where they'd be, now. Filed away somewhere."

"It's okay." Yvonne smiled. "I'm sure we can get the information from archives and the web." She pulled photographs from her bag and handed them to Mark. "Do you recognise any of these people? The pictures were taken here, at your hotel. Do you remember anything?"

He pointed to the newest of the photographs. "Abuse survivors group. They meet here every few years. These were the people who came together to comfort each other and look for ways forward."

"Were they trying to get the investigation reopened?"

"No. Nothing like that. At least, not the survivors. They avoided publicity like the plague. Or, at least, some of them did. I remember her." He tapped his finger on the image of Kate Nilsson. "She's not one of them."

"No?"

"No. I got talking to her. Probably the night that picture was taken, I'd say. She was sat at the bar. Shoulders hunched and chin in her hands. I felt sorry for her and joined her for a while."

"What was troubling her?" Yvonne stared at him intently.

"She'd had a row with one of the survivors. A fellow soldier, I think she said. One of her friends."

"What was that row about?"

"She didn't go into detail, but she said she wished the person would let her go public. I wondered if it was something to do with the abuse, but she was cryptic about it. Not really giving me anything to go on. She was very sad. She looked about ready to give up."

Yvonne shifted in her chair. "Did she say who it was she'd rowed with?"

"No, she didn't."

"I see."

"She's a lovely girl. I'd love to meet her again." He gave a wistful smile.

"I'm afraid that won't be possible." The DI's eyes were downcast. "She's dead." She let out a slow sigh.

"Dead?" The shock in his face appeared to be genuine. "How? Why?"

"She was murdered in cold blood. Assassinated, in effect."

He put a hand to his mouth, which had opened as though to say more. Nothing came.

"I'm sorry to tell you like this."

"I hadn't expected that." He shook his head. "Is that why you're here?"

"It is."

"I wish I could tell you more."

The DI reached out to put a hand on his shoulder. "You've given us quite a bit. Could we trouble you for the guest list, from the time Kate was here? Would you be able to find it for us?"

He thought for a moment. "Of course. It'll take me about half an hour, but I run a pretty tight ship, as regards records. It'll be here."

The DI rewarded him with a broad smile.

FOUR NAMES JUMPED out at them:

Kate Nilsson

Stephen Whyte

Wayne Hedges

Billy Rawlins.

It suggested that Stephen Whyte, Wayne Hedges and

Billy Rawlins were possible survivors of abuse at Sunnymede children's home. The older photographs which Kate had had in her possession pointed to Scotty McEwan, Helen Reynolds and Tom Rendon as also being survivors of abuse at that home. Albeit their abuse had happened a few years earlier.

"Was that what Kate was onto?" Yvonne felt sure this information was key. "Billy Rawlins..." She pursed her lips, shaking her head, as Dewi began the drive back. "Billy Rawlins is the surprise. His abuse must have occurred not long before the home was closed for good. He's not old enough for anything else. Boy, there's so much to get my head around."

Yvonne felt deep concern for Billy. "We've got to find him," she said, as they arrived back. "He told me he warned Kate off looking into the Dale deaths. He knows something."

A quick phone call to Dale confirmed that Billy Rawlins had not yet returned. Broderick Forster explained to Yvonne that he wasn't overly concerned, yet. This was not the first time Billy had gone AWOL.

"He suffers panic attacks. He's received counselling." Forster's tone was clipped and to the point. "He's risking medical discharge."

Yvonne identified with the panic attacks. "How many times has he done this?" she asked.

"This is the third time in three years."

The DI sighed. "Can you let us know if he returns?"

"Yes. Of course." Forster's line clicked and went dead.

YVONNE TASKED Dai Clayton and Callum Jones with looking through online news archives for information about

Sunnymede and the alleged abuse. She was surprised at the extent of the allegations. The majority had either been unsuccessfully prosecuted or not prosecuted at all. The accused had included politicians, celebrities, police officers, and other pillars of the community. The list was staggering. Strings of people going to and from the home.

She sat back in her chair, pensive. Dewi plopped down two fresh coffees on the desk. "Do you think this is the key?" he asked, as he pulled up another chair.

"Honestly? I don't know, Dewi. But, I think it could be." She blew on the top of her coffee before taking a grateful sip. "Stephen Whyte told me to look at the battalion sergeants and then keep going up. But how high? Commanders? MOD? Politicians?"

"But if he knew they were all victims of abuse, as he had been, why didn't he tell you that? Why be so cryptic about it?"

"I think we got our answer to that when he was killed, Dewi. I suspect, as well, that he was trying to protect others."

"Such as Billy Rawlins?"

"I think so. And Wayne Hedges…"

"Who knew you were going to meet Corporal Whyte?" Dewi took several swift gulps of his coffee, as though his mouth was made of asbestos. The DI was still blowing on hers. "No one. I don't think…no, wait. Wayne Hedges. Wayne knew."

"Might he have passed that on to someone?"

Yvonne pursed her lips. "Possible, I guess." She thought back to when she'd first met Wayne. He'd seemed nervous and scared. "But if he did, I think he would have done so inadvertently. I say we go back to Lars Nilsson. If Kate knew all about the abuse connection and the soldiers who died, then you can bet her journalist father knew, too."

"Perhaps that's the part of the story he wanted most of all." Dewi finished his drink.

"Perhaps it's part of the reason Hayley Nilsson is so nervous. Powerful people might do anything to avoid being exposed."

"Looks like T.H.Davis won't be much help." Dewi pointed to the paragraph in the summary which outlined Davis' dementia. "He joined the Lords, only to be retired a couple of years later."

"We could talk to the guy who ran the place. He's in HMP Altcourse. Ask one of the DCs to arrange something."

"Will do, ma'am."

BILLY RAWLINS THREW his bedroll down onto the floor of his makeshift shelter. He'd spent the last hour or two arranging branches and leaves, the way he'd been taught. He checked his watch. Four-thirty and getting too dark to work without a torch.

He lit his hexamine stove. It gave off just enough heat to have a hot drink and some food. He didn't want to risk a full fire.

He put his pan of water on the stove and went back inside his shelter, to check his map by torchlight.

He wasn't even sure what he was running from. Just knew it was evil. He could feel its thick, sinuous tendrils reaching out for him. The darkness was sweeping every-thing before it. He'd felt it first when he was a boy. Then, he had felt that if he got out of bed, he would fall off the earth. Only his sheets kept him safe. And then again, in Afghanistan. It waited for him outside the walls of Camp Bastion. And now, somewhere out there, it lurked again. He wasn't going to wait for it to get to him.

16

LARS OPENS UP

Yvonne and Dewi waited patiently outside Lars and Hayley Nilsson's home. They'd heard movement. Footsteps on the stairs. Someone was coming.

Lars Nilsson opened the door, expectancy lining his tired face.

"I'm sorry, did we wake you?" Yvonne meant it. She did feel sorry. It was clear the man hadn't slept much.

He rubbed his forehead. "I was dozing. We had a bad night." He glanced at Dewi, before shifting his gaze back to the DI. "Has there been a development? Have you found my daughter's killer?"

Yvonne shook her head. "I'm sorry, not yet."

His face fell, his bloodshot eyes half-closed. "Then why-"

"We wanted to ask about your daughter's investigation into the deaths at the barracks. May we come in? Or should we come back at a better time?"

Lars stepped back into his hallway, running a hand through his hair before motioning them inside. "Come into the kitchen. We'll need to keep our voices down. My wife has only just gotten off to sleep, too. She needs her rest."

"I understand." Yvonne nodded.

Lars arranged seats next to the Aga. The DI was glad of its warmth. She saw Dewi reach his hands behind his chair to touch it. Giving them a rub, after he'd held them there a few seconds.

"So, how can I help?" Lars rubbed his eyes and leaned back in his chair, his voice low and cracked.

"You know your daughter was looking into the deaths at the Dale barracks."

"Yes."

"Did she mention that many of the victims were also victims of abuse?"

Lars paused, mouth partially open. She could see the knowledge in his sunken eyes.

"Can I ask when you knew?"

He let out a large puff of air. "From the beginning. Pretty much from the beginning of her investigation. Some of her friends had been victims. She went to a survivors get-together."

"But she wasn't a survivor of abuse?"

"No. She'd gone along to support Wayne and Stephen, among others. That was just after she found out. I think she found out accidentally, by overhearing an argument between Wayne and Stephen."

Yvonne pursed her lips before whispering, "Why didn't you tell us this before? You want your daughter's murder solved?"

Lars bowed his head, gazing at the tiles on the kitchen floor. "I do."

"Then why?"

"Guilt." He let out a heavy sigh. A tear dropped off the end of his nose.

"Guilt? I don't understand." The DI kept her voice soft.

"The sexual abuse scandal at Sunnymede had been on my radar for years. When I found out that some of the survivors had been found dead at Dale, I was excited at the possibility of investigating both stories at once."

"And you had someone on the inside."

"I did." Lars let out a painful sob which wracked his body. "It was my idea. I asked Kate if she would help. I put my own daughter into the dragon's mouth. I have to live with that. It's something I will always carry. I don't know if I will ever sleep again. I don't deserve to."

"Lars, I'm sure Kate would not have taken on the investigation, unless she, too, had wanted the answers." She resisted the urge to put a hand on his shoulder. "Some of her friends were victims. She would have wanted to do it for them."

He looked up at her. She sensed doubt. He was stifling the urge to say something.

"You know who the killer is?"

He shook his head.

"But you think Kate knew?"

"I strongly believe she knew."

"What makes you so sure?"

"She was different when she came home this time. She seemed dejected. I went up to her room, a couple of days before she died. She was slamming things around, muttering about being let down. She was angry with someone."

"A friend?"

"That's the impression I got."

"So, let me get this straight. You think one of Kate's friends may have been involved in the deaths at Dale?"

"It's a suspicion, yes. I think the deaths on the base are linked to the abuse that went on at Sunnymede. I think that before she died, my daughter figured out who was responsible. Whoever that person was had Kate killed, or killed her themselves."

"And that is why your wife was afraid of you talking to me."

Lars nodded. "We may none-of-us be safe."

YVONNE TURNED to Dewi as they left the house. "Wayne and Billy are in danger. We've got to locate both of them. I think one of them is the killer."

"Ma'am?" Dewi raised his eyebrows.

"Kate had her suspicions, but didn't tell anyone. Not even her father. Why not? I told Wayne Hedges I wanted to meet Stephen Whyte."

"We need to find Billy." Dewi agreed.

THE CHASE

Yvonne could feel the sweat developing on her brow, as she fought to find her phone in her handbag. Instinct told her she couldn't afford to miss this call.

"Hello? Inspector?" It was Billy Rawlins.

"Billy? Yes, this is Inspector Giles. Billy, where are you?"

"There're after me. They're coming, I haven't got long."

"Who's after you, Billy? Billy?"

There were huffing and scraping sounds in the background. She heard the creak of a door. There was brief birdsong then silence, save for the occasional muffled car. This was followed by beeping. The line went dead.

"Was that Billy Rawlins?" Dewi took the phone from the shocked DI, and wrote down the number from the last received call.

"It was." Yvonne sparked into action. "He's in danger and that sounded like a phone box."

"Should be easy for the lads to trace." Dewi was already dialling through to Newtown station, using his own mobile. He barked instruction to Callum Jones and Dai Clayton.

Then it was a case of waiting. They leaned on the car, in the middle of LLydiart, every muscle in their bodies taut. They wanted to go go go. But without knowing where to, they were left listening to the birds and drumming their fingers.

"THE CALL CAME from a BT box on the edge of Plas Power Woods, near Bersham." The unusually high pitch of Callum's voice, betrayed his excitement, as he gave Dewi the GPS coordinates.

"That's near Wrexham." Dewi frowned. "We're gonna need backup. Get on to North Wales Police. Tell them what's going on. We've got an individual on the run in the area, who believes he's in danger. The assailant or assailants may be armed and *will* be dangerous."

"Have you spoken to the DCI?" Callum hesitated.

"No time. I'm heading up there with the DI. Ask Dai Clayton to get on to Dale Barracks and find out if Wayne Hedges is on the base. Get back to us as soon as you know one way or the other.'

"Will do."

"Oh, and Callum?"

"Yep?"

"When you call back, ring Yvonne's phone. I'm driving."

"Will do."

"Let's go." Yvonne was breathless as she threw open the passenger door and fumbled with the seat belt.

"We're off to Bersham, ma'am."

"Put your foot down. Use your lights and sirens if you have to."

.   .   .

THEY WERE NEARLY twenty minutes into the journey, when Yvonne got a call from Callum. "What have you got?" she asked, heart pounding.

"Forster's had his men looking all over. Wayne Hedges is not on the base and no one knows where he is. He missed roll call this morning. He hasn't been seen since lunchtime, yesterday."

"Thanks, Callum. Can you pass this on to North Wales. Let them know they are dealing with an experienced soldier who may be armed. Ask them to go careful, we don't know for sure that he's armed or what we are facing. We're going to get there as soon as we can. I've got to find Billy. He knows me, and I think he trusts me."

"Okay. Ma'am?"

"Yes, Callum?"

"Take it steady. Don't do anything daft."

"Thanks, Callum."

Yvonne filled Dewi in, as the car sped ever closer to their destination. She kept her phone in her hand, in case Billy tried calling again.

Another twenty minutes and they were approaching the woods. Dewi parked in a lay-by to program the GPS coordinates. "We're close. Another mile, I reckon." He fired up the engine, again. The DI had to remind herself to breath.

THEY FOUND THE CALL BOX. It was actually a wifi and call-charging box. Yvonne opened the kiosk door and found the phone as it had been left, the receiver hanging down.

She stepped back out and scanned the tree-line and road in both directions.

"See anything?" Dewi joined her, checking he'd got his cuffs and pepper spray.

"Phone off the hook and dangling. He left in a hurry, that's for sure. Question is, was anyone with him. God, I hope he's all right."

Dewi took a call from Callum. "Sir, back up is being sorted. It's been delayed as the DCI wanted to know exactly what was going on. He's organising it himself. He's talking to North Wales now. He wants you to hold back and wait for their arrival."

"Okay. Thanks, Callum."

"What did he say, Dewi?" Yvonne was busy putting her boots on. She looked up, when Dewi didn't answer straight away. "Well? What's wrong?"

"DCI wants us to hold off. We've got to wait here until back up arrives."

"What? Why isn't back up in place already? Look, you stay here. I'm just going to head into the trees over there and see if I can see anything."

"If he's in the woods, he could be anywhere in there. Anyway, there's no way I'm letting you go in alone."

"Then let's go."

They climbed over the gate and onto the frozen ground. The DI was glad of her scarf, which she had wound tightly. She suspected the temperature was below zero. Her breath made large clouds of steam.

They headed into the tree-line, separated by about fifteen feet.

"What was that?" Dewi looked off to his left, and they listened intently.

"Can't hear anything."

"Thought I heard twigs snapping." Dewi resumed moving forward.

They followed a small stream, the going increasingly difficult, as there were fallen trees and a fair amount of undergrowth which badly needed cutting back. They had been walking for about fifteen minutes, when another loud snapping came from somewhere to their left. Dewi barked at the DI to stay back and he headed to where the noise had come from. Yvonne was about to ignore his instruction and follow, when a wooden shack caught her attention. She glanced over at Dewi's disappearing back, and headed over to the shack, pepper spray in hand.

She peered through the tiny window. It was empty, but someone had been there recently. There were several beer cans, some unopened. Remnants of food, on a plate on the floor, lay next to a sleeping bag. Yvonne glanced behind her but Dewi had disappeared. She tried the door to the shack. It wasn't locked but the door was swollen and stiff. She managed to get it open and gingerly checked among the few things on the floor. They included a small, hexamine stove. The kind used by hardcore campers or the army.

Fear gripped her body and she took several deep breaths. Billy -and or Wayne- was close by. She knew it. She took another deep breath before heading back to the shack door.

Dewi was still nowhere to be seen. She listened, afraid to call in case she brought unwanted attention to her DS or herself. She heard sirens in the distance. That had to be the back up. She decided to check a little further downstream, buoyed by the knowledge help had arrived and would soon be on site.

There were voices, coming from just beyond the tiny dell in front. She strained to hear but got only snatches and couldn't make out what was being said. She struggled down a bank, and headed to where she thought the voices were coming from.

She froze. Just below her, at the bottom of a small ravine, were Billy Rawlins and Wayne Hedges. Hedges had his arm raised. He was aiming a pistol at Billy, who was backing up, his hands raised, repeatedly saying, 'No'.

She hid behind a tree, her back to it, and called out. "Wayne. Wayne, wait." She couldn't see his reaction, but Billy had stopped speaking. There was silence. She continued, "Wayne, you're surrounded. North Wales Police have their ARV team in place. They'll shoot you on sight, if you're holding or you use that weapon."

"Come out, or I'll shoot him." Wayne's voice cut through her heavy breathing.

She heard another voice.

"Ma'am?" It was Dewi.

"Stay back, Dewi," she called out, fearful her DS would be shot, before he even realised what was happening.

"Come out!" Wayne ordered.

She closed her eyes, holding a deep breath for a second before releasing it. She raised her hands and walked from behind the tree.

"Keep walking," Wayne ordered again.

She slipped, barely managing to control her decent down into the ravine. She used one of her hands to get her balance, and tore it on a bramble.

Wayne alternately aimed the gun at her and at Billy, as the three of them stood, triangulated. The DI could feel panic rising through her, but the fear was more for Billy than herself.

"Ma'am, no." Dewi was somewhere behind her.

"Keep walking,' Wayne directed. He appeared unsure, as

though not certain of where he was going to take things. Billy saw his chance, and made a run for it.

Wayne turned the gun from the DI and levelled it at Billy, who was weaving, hampered by the sides of the ravine and the undergrowth.

The gun rang out. Billy dropped.

"No!" Yvonne started towards Billy.

"Stay where you are are." Wayne once more had the gun on her.

She paused, tears running down her face. "Wayne, don't do this. Let me help Billy."

Wayne was also choked with emotion. She could see the tremor in his arm holding the gun. "Why did you have to come asking questions?" he blurted at her.

"Because you killed Kate. You killed her in cold blood." Her heart banged in her rib cage. Her knuckles white in her tightly-clenched hands.

Wayne let out a pained howl, gun still aimed at Yvonne. "She wouldn't leave it. She wouldn't leave it alone. I asked her to back off and she wouldn't listen."

Yvonne breathed deep. "She wanted those who hurt you to be punished for what they did."

"You think that helps?" His face contorted. "You think that helps? Making us victims all over again? In the papers. On the telly. We are accused of being money-grabbers. Of wanting fifteen minutes of fame. They don't care what happens to us." He waved the gun, wildly. "They just want stories to sell their papers and fatten their viewing figures. The abusers get off scot-free. They get to remember the fun they had and they get off scot-free. They just fucking protect each other." He spat onto the ground. "I don't want to be in the papers. I don't want to be seen as a victim or as someone after money. Those bastards hurt us. Every one of us. Who cared? Who cares now?"

"Kate cared. And Billy. What did Billy do? He's lying down there hurt. He was abused too. Now you've just hurt him again."

"Shut up. Just shut up. You don't know what you're talking about. He would have talked."

"Wayne," Yvonne held her hands out in front of her, palms towards him. "Police are all around this place. They're everywhere. Why don't you put the gun down. Please, please, put the gun down." She glanced to her right, where she'd last seen Dewi. He was crouched, talking into his mobile. Her eyes turned back to Wayne.

He walked towards her. Gun still aimed at her.

"Did you kill Scotty McEwan?"

He stopped in his tracks, his eyes dripping hatred. "I didn't kill Scotty. They destroyed him."

"He had everything to live for."

"He played the game. He tried to make the best of it. He had the swagger, but inside he was dying. I knew it. I could see it. Anyone who really knew him, knew that. I didn't kill him. He would never have exposed us. He felt the same way I do."

"And Tom Rendon?"

"Scotty's death ripped him up. I don't know what happened to Tom. The people who run everything, who control everything, they use us. They use us all. Can't you see that? I don't want to wear their mark. I shook it off." He let out a sob.

Yvonne wanted to go to him. He had the appearance of a small child. Lost. "Let me go to Billy, please."

"No." He raised the gun once more and she heard him pull the hammer back.

A shot rang out. "Go. Go. Go."

Wayne fell to his knees in the dirt, before falling forward, face-down onto the frozen ground.

"No. No. No." Yvonne's whole body shook. It took her a moment to fully register what had happened. Armoured police officers poured into the ravine. Medical personnel rushed to Billy and Wayne.

She sat on the cold ground, hands either side of her head, and stayed there for several minutes. The trees around her spun and she felt as though she might faint. She tried to get up, but her legs felt weak.

Dewi came rushing to her side.

She broke down on his shoulder. Huge sobs which wracked her body. "It wasn't supposed to end like this."

"Billy's alive." Dewi put a hand either side of her head. "Billy's been shot in the chest. He's got a collapsed lung, but he'll make it."

Her eyes searched his face. "Really? Thank God."

She looked back towards Wayne. He was lying as he fell. Ambulance staff were removing the equipment they had been using to test for life. They backed off and police moved in. It was now officially a crime scene.

AFTERMATH

Yvonne was seated alone on a bench in Dolerw Park, not far from the station. She could see the river bubbling away below her and could hear the children in the playground at Hafren School to her left. The laughter and squeals of the innocent.

She kept seeing Wayne Hedges, his face in pain. His anger with people and life in general.

"Penny for your thoughts?" Tasha took a seat next to her.

It was the first time the DI had smiled in days. "Tasha."

"You look troubled."

"We found the killer."

"I know. Dewi told me. He also told me you're still coming to terms with it all." Tasha's eyes searched the DI's face.

"We have to protect them better."

"Protect who?" Tasha asked, her voice hushed.

"Our children." She turned her face towards the excited voices. "Monsters aren't born, they're made. They're fashioned from the young and the innocent."

"For the most part," Tasha nodded, "I can't argue with that."

"Did Dewi tell you the reasons Kate and Stephen's killer gave? The reasons for doing what he did?" Yvonne bought her eyes to Tasha's.

"He mentioned it, yes."

"He killed them because he didn't want people to know he was abused." She shook her head. "He wanted to hide it from the world so badly. I still don't fully understand why he would have gone to such lengths. Why didn't he just support Kate in her fight for justice and ask for his name to be left out of it?"

Tasha pursed her lips. "Obviously, I can't say for sure, but his being abused probably clashed with his sense of himself as a man and as a soldier. He may have chosen a traditionally macho career as his way of fighting back. Of forgetting what he had been through. He built himself a fortress. The story coming out threatened to destroy that fortress and expose him as a victim. Something he had worked so hard to prevent."

"He went to a survivors reunion."

"So did Kate. So did a lot of people who were there to support others. He may not have known until he went to the group that it wasn't for him. Besides, didn't you say Kate's father was a journalist? Even if Wayne trusted Kate, he may not have trusted her father."

"She didn't deserve to die."

"No, she didn't."

"Neither did Stephen Whyte."

"You saved Billy Rawlins."

"I very nearly didn't."

"You're wallowing again."

Yvonne sighed. "I'm sorry. This case has been gruelling for everyone. I still can't help wondering about the other deaths at the barracks. What really happened to those soldiers? And how does that tie in with what happened to Kate? I think it's time I talked frankly with Harold Thornton." Yvonne rose purposefully from her seat.

"Can I come?" Tasha moved to join her.

"I don't see why not. Thornton and his sidekick are due at the station later today."

"Why don't we take Dewi for lunch and fortify ourselves for the task."

"Good idea." Yvonne smiled. "Somehow, you always manage to pull me out of it."

Tasha grinned. "It's what friends are for."

"THANK you for coming here again to see me." Yvonne paused in the doorway.

Thornton shrugged. "It's a good opportunity to tie up loose ends. We're officially closing the case our end." He'd waited for her in the coffee area, and was seated on an armless, soft chair.

Her eyes wandered to his unusually loose tie and open top button. He caught her looking and she cleared her throat noisily, giving him a stern look. "I wanted to ask about the deaths at Dale. The ones Kate Nilsson was interested in: Scotty McEwan, Helen Reynolds and Tom Rendon." She took a seat adjacent to his.

He looked at her for a good two seconds, and she was unsure whether he was going to oblige. He rubbed his chin, finally. "Fire away. What do you want to know?"

Yvonne leaned towards him. "You found that the deaths were suicides or accidents, and I'm struggling with that."

"How so?" He narrowed his eyes.

"Scotty's family said he was several times over the limit. They want to know how he got up that tree to hang himself. They don't believe he did."

"I see." He pursed his lips, and placed his hands together as though in prayer, tapping them against his chin. "Let me tell you about those deaths. I really want to clear it up for you." He leaned back in his chair. "They were all of them damaged. Each of them to a different degree. Helen was angry. Angry at everyone, and determined not to lose her spirit. That spurred on the officers. They were every bit as determined to break her as she was determined never to break. It got out of control. She should have told them she was overheating but her pride wouldn't let her."

"What about Scotty? How did he hang himself from that tree, drunk?"

"I'm sure you know that young men, when drunk, can do some pretty amazing and dangerous things. Climbing up tall scaffolds, for instance."

Yvonne looked away.

"Scotty was a soldier. He threw the rope over the branch. Looped it. Climbed up it. Then hung himself. Soldiers can do that. Scotty had tried out with the SAS. He'd failed, but his fitness was never in question."

"And the marks in the field? The ones that were washed away?"

"They'd been there from several days prior to Scotty's death. A team of guys were surveying the area. They'd set up their tripods there. It's likely the prints were from their exploits."

"And Tom Rendon?"

"PTSD. Everything he'd been through. He hadn't just lost Scotty. He'd seen one of his other best mates blown to bits by an IED in Helmand province."

Yvonne leaned back in her chair. It dawned on her that, by the end, Kate was probably more interested in the sexual abuse of those soldiers as youngsters, than she was in their deaths. She had wanted the perpetrators properly punished. Perhaps one day they would be. She shook her head. "So much tragedy."

"It was hard, investigating those deaths. It took a lot out of myself and Richard. The army learned a lot, you know. Things have and are changing. It *is* getting better."

Yvonne smiled, sadly, at Thornton. "I misjudged you."

Thornton smiled back. "You're forgiven. It's healthy to analyse everything you are told, in your job...and in ours. I wasn't overly surprised by your scepticism."

"Friends?"

Thornton grinned. "Friends."

THE CHILDREN WHOOPED and Kim gave a broad smile as they opened the door to Yvonne. She had an arm full of presents and yet more gifts -food and alcohol- in the car.

Her mother stood behind, her eyes searching her daughter's face.

As soon as she was inside and relieved of her load, Yvonne crossed the floor to hold her mother. They stood, hugging for what must have been five minutes. Hot tears falling down the DI's face.

"Merry Christmas," she said, before breaking away and finding her mother's present.

Her mum appeared as though she had won the lottery.

Years of worry and guilt falling away. "Merry Christmas, Yvonne. I love you," was all she said.

THE END

AFTERWORD

If you enjoyed this book, I'd be very grateful if you'd post a short review on Amazon. Your support really does make a difference and helps bring my books to more readers like you.

Mailing list: You can join my emailing list here : AnnamarieMorgan.com

Facebook page: AnnamarieMorganAuthor

You might also like to read the other books in the series:
Book 1: Death Master:
After months of mental and physical therapy, Yvonne Giles, an Oxford DI, is back at work and that's just how she likes it. So when she's asked to hunt the serial killer responsible for taking apart young women, the DI jumps at the chance but hides the fact she is suffering debilitating flashbacks. She is told to work with Tasha Phillips, an in-her-face, criminal psychologist. The DI is not enamoured with the idea. Tasha has a lot to prove. Yvonne has a lot to get over. A tentative link with a 20 year-old cold case brings

them closer to the truth but events then take a horrifyingly personal turn.

Book 2: You Will Die

After apprehending an Oxford Serial Killer, and almost losing her life in the process, DI Yvonne Giles has left England for a quieter life in rural Wales.Her peace is shattered when she is asked to hunt a priest-killing psychopath, who taunts the police with messages inscribed on the corpses.Yvonne requests the help of Dr. Tasha Phillips, a psychologist and friend, to aid in the hunt. But the killer is one step ahead and the ultimatum, he sets them, could leave everyone devastated.

Book 3: Total Wipeout

A whole family is wiped out with a shotgun. At first glance, it's an open-and-shut case. The dad did it, then killed himself. The deaths follow at least two similar family wipeouts – attributed to the financial crash.

So why doesn't that sit right with Detective Inspector Yvonne Giles? And why has a rape occurred in the area, in the weeks preceding each family's demise? Her seniors do not believe there are questions to answer. DI Giles must therefore risk everything, in a high-stakes investigation ofa mysterious masonic ring and players in high finance.

Can she find the answers, before the next innocent family is wiped out?

Book 4: Deep Cut

In a tiny hamlet in North Wales, a female recruit is murdered whilst on Christmas home leave. Detective Inspector Yvonne Giles is asked to cut short her own leave, to investigate. Why was the young soldier killed? And is her death related to several alleged suicides at her army base? DI Giles this it is, and that someone powerful has a dark secret they will do anything to hide.

Book 5: The Pusher

Young men are turning up dead on the banks of the River Severn. Some of them have been missing for days or even weeks. The only thing the police can be sure of, is that the men have drowned. Rumours abound that a mythical serial killer has turned his attention from the Manchester canal to the waterways of Mid-Wales. And now one of CID's own is missing. A brand new recruit with everything to live for. DI Giles must find him before it's too late.

Book 6: Gone

Children are going missing. They are not heard from again until sinister requests for cryptocurrency go viral. The public must pay or the children die. For lead detective Yvonne Giles, the case is complicated enough. And then the unthinkable happens...

Book 7: Bone Dancer

A serial killer is murdering women, threading their bones back together, and leaving them for police to find. Detective Inspector Yvonne Giles must find him before more innocent victims die. Problem is, the killer wants her and will do anything he can to get her. Unaware that she, herself, is is a target, DI Giles risks everything to catch him.

Book 8: Blood Lost

A young man comes home to find his whole family missing. Half-eaten breakfasts and blood spatter on the lounge wall are the only clues to what happened...

Book 9: Angel of Death

He is watching. Biding his time. Preparing himself for a torturous kill. Soaring above; lord of all. His journey, direct through the lives of the unsuspecting.

The Angel of Death is nigh.

The peace of the Mid-Wales countryside is shattered, when a female eco-warrior is found crucified in a public wood. At first, it would appear a simple case of finding which of the woman's enemies had had her killed. But DI Yvonne Giles has no idea how bad things are going to get. As the body count rises, she will need all of her instincts, and the skills of those closest to her, to stop the murderous rampage of the Angel of Death.

Book 10: Death in the Air

Several fatal air collisions have occurred within a few months in rural Wales. According to the local Air Accidents Investigation Branch (AAIB) inspector, it's a coincidence. Clusters happen. Except, this cluster is different. DI Yvonne Giles suspects it when she hears some of the witness statements but, when an AAIB inspector is found dead under a bridge, she knows it.

Something is way off. Yvonne is determined to get to the bottom of the mystery, but exactly how far down the treacherous rabbit hole is she prepared to go?

Book 11: Death in the Mist

The morning after a viscous sea-mist covers the seaside town of Aberystwyth, a young student lies brutalised within one hundred yards of the castle ruins.

DI Yvonne Giles' reputation precedes her. Having successfully captured more serial killers than some detectives have caught colds, she is seconded to head the murder investigation team, and hunt down the young woman's killer.

What she doesn't know, is this is only the beginning...

Book 12: Death under Hypnosis

When the secretive and mysterious Sheila Winters approaches Yvonne Giles and tells her that she murdered someone thirty years before, she has the DI's immediate attention.

Things get even more strange when Sheila states:

She doesn't know who.

She doesn't know where.

She doesn't know why.

Book 13: Fatal Turn

A seasoned hiker goes missing from the Dolfor Moors after recording a social media video describing a narrow cave he intends to explore. A tragic accident? Nothing to see here, until a team of cavers disappear on a coastal potholing expedition, setting off a string of events that has DI Giles tearing her hair out. What, or who is the thread that ties this series of disappearances together?

A serial killer, thriller murder-mystery set in Wales.

Book 14: The Edinburgh Murders

A newly retired detective from the Met is murdered in a murky alley in Edinburgh, a sinister calling card left with the body.

The dead man had been a close friend of psychologist Tasha Phillips, giving her her first gig with the Met decades before.

Tasha begs DI Yvonne Giles to aid the Scottish police in solving the case.

In unfamiliar territory, and with a ruthless killer haunting the streets, the DI plunges herself into one of the darkest, most terrifying cases of her career. Who exactly is The Poet?

Remember to watch out for Book 15, coming soon...

Printed in Great Britain
by Amazon